Cindy M. Amos

SANCTIFYING ACE AERIALIST

Landscapes of Mercy, Book 4

By Cindy M. Amos

For in the day of trouble,

He will keep me safe in his dwelling;

He will hide me in the shelter of His sanctuary

And set me high upon a rock.

Psalm 27:5

Cindy M. Amos

Copyright © 2017 by Cindy M. Amos
Published by Forget Me Not Romances, a division of Winged Publications

ISBN-13:978-1-944203-95-5

Dedicated to my sheltering husband Jay M. Amos

For introducing me to Pawnee Rock, Kansas

The author would like to acknowledge the following
for their support and encouragement with this book:
istock cover photograph of Pawnee Rock, KS
Pamela Bower, Proofreader
Janice Fairbairn, Marketing Strategist for LOM Series
Members of the South Central Kansas ACFW Chapter
Cynthia Hickey of Forget Me Not Romances
& Inspiration of the Holy Spirit

LANDSCAPES OF MERCY SERIES BOOK FOUR

Yet there is one ray of hope:
God's compassion never ends.
Only the Lord's mercies have kept us
from complete destruction.
Great is His faithfulness;
His lovingkindness renews each day.
Lamentations 3:21-23

Chapter 1

An exodus always looked more like a meander to her when viewed from the backside. From the trash-rimmed main parking lot of Tanah Keeta Wildlife Park, Paisley St. James bit back the bile of regret. She had reluctance at accepting the departure of the Re-Occupy movement that had livened things up considerably in their remote burg of Pawnee Rock, Kansas. A mere football field's distance from the original Santa Fe Trail, it seemed as though the wagon train had passed by the town once again, its prairie schooner sails set for greener pastures. Noticing her helper seemed to be having a problem with their final task of the day, she headed for the port-o-lets as the waste disposal company had arrived on schedule for their retrieval.

Her bulky co-worker rattled the door of the last unit, but couldn't get it open. "Hey, we're still occupied." He gave a tired laugh.

"Kurtis Morehead, you're complicating my escape," she replied, hands on hips. When he shrugged his broad shoulders and yielded access, she grabbed the door.

About that time, a guttural retch sounded from within and her helper recoiled, making a sour face. The truck backed into position to load the first unit and Paisley tossed the driver a wave. A second glance at the door confirmed her helper's suspicion. It read "occupied."

"Come on out, buddy. The party's over." She waited for a response, her foot tamping the pavement. In a quick assessment of the cleanup work around the campsite, she spotted a heap of gear under the far honey locust tree. Maybe it matched the occupant.

Kurtis wandered over to help the driver load the pink port-o-let on the far end.

"Leave me behind," a voice inside demanded in a solitary exhalation.

A cutting quip came to mind, but before she could utter it a muffled gag echoed out of the outhouse's upper vent. Guilt stabbed her in the Christian charity zone of her heart. Maybe some compassion would be in order.

"Listen friend, you've already been left behind. Your people departed the premises over half an hour ago. I'm your new people and here's my dilemma. The waste disposal service is here to take their rental units back, including the one you're occupying." She took a breath and watched the truck shift in front of the second pink unit. Down to half a minute, she had to come up with something to crowbar that door open and free up the unit.

"Come on, buddy. You don't want to be in the splash zone when this thing gets hoisted, take my word for it. Trust me, we're good people. We can help you get back on your feet. You can catch up to your Re-Occupy group later if you want." The sound of the second unit dropping into place on the flatbed truck crushed any response that might have come.

The driver inched the truck toward her with a questioning look on his scruffy face as Kurtis stood beside the third unit. The loading crane slid over the housing as an imminent threat.

In the instant, she heard a faint click as the door sign in front of her rotated to "vacant." Doubling her ponytail to keep her hair out of harm's way, she squared her shoulders to better catch the ailing vagrant as he emerged. She held her breath as the door began to swing open.

A wavy mat of tousled black hair led a hunched man from the unit, hands locked on his thighs as he stepped out. He let out a continuous groan.

Unsure how much help to offer, she froze arms-up in front of him and couldn't believe her eyes. The discarded member happened to be the animated leader of the group, the fiery speaker she'd overheard yesterday at quitting time.

"Leave me behind," he repeated in a weak voice as his body pitched forward toward the pavement.

She jammed her hands under his arms in a rescuer's grip as he went limp as a noodle. Before she had to make a decision whether to become his collision mat or not, Kurtis stepped in and diverted the extra weight off her knees.

She straightened and glimpsed the parking lot. "Head for your truck." She nodded to the east curb. "I'll grab his gear and use it to pad the bed."

Kurtis hoisted the sick man over his shoulder in a fireman's carry and took a few ginger steps toward his vehicle.

In a run, she assessed the trash around the perimeter and glanced at the trees to judge the wind speed. Waiting a day would make the cleanup twice as time-consuming once left to the Kansas wind's dispersal habits, but people came first, especially incapacitated ones. What choice did she have? She shouldered the man's backpack into place, hefted the remaining gear in one grab, and made a beeline for the truck.

Kurtis had the tailgate down and the sick man coiled reactively halfway into the bed. Scrambling past him, she unfolded the tent and made a makeshift pallet, motioning for Kurtis to load the patient. He came to her headfirst, and when he plopped down, she fell between him and the tent. Not waiting to see if she wanted to be there, Kurtis flung himself behind the wheel and cranked the ignition. "To Leta's house?" he asked out of the lowering window.

Essence of musty tent overcame her. She situated the heavy head more comfortably in her lap and gave their destination some consideration. "Yeah, Leta's," she replied with mixed feelings. Not that the aging saint couldn't nurse this fellow back to health, as the woman had never met a stray cat she didn't like to plump up. Maybe the fact that she lived in Leta's upstairs apartment made it hit a little too close to home for her. She wouldn't be shed of her new problem quite that easily.

Her lap lump shifted, coiling into a helpless fetal position. His eyes opened involuntarily to reveal the deepest blue pools imaginable.

"I'm Paisley," she said, attempting to humanize the experience. His mouth opened without his lips moving and she brushed a matted mess out of his ample black hair. The softness of it caused a sensation she wasn't expecting. Regret soon poked her in the ribs.

"Paisley? No wonder I see swirls," he replied, his lips closing in a grimace.

When she chuckled, the regret vanished—a nice gift for a rescuer. The truck lurched and she wondered if Kurtis always drove like this, jumping curbs and swerving at road kill. At long last, her street appeared through the back glass. She sighed and tried not to think about how blown her evening would be, now that she was bringing home a member of the Re-Occupy movement. Civil protest never respected the clock or calendar anyhow. A vicious stomach growl sounded from the coiled up left behind leader, leading her diagnosis to pinpoint something he'd eaten.

"Must be hard to live without the modern convenience of refrigeration." Her observation solicited a moan that lacked humor. She placed a hand on his forehead and checked for fever, realizing Leta would soon be asking. Her take on his local forecast was clammy but cool, with a strong possibility of future digestive eruptions. "We're taking you to Miss Leta's house. She's den mother for the whole village and will handle you with TLC. I live right upstairs, so we'll tag-team until you're on your feet again. How does that sound?"

He gave a weak nod.

The truck popped up a driveway and she noticed that Kurtis had pulled into her usual spot. The day didn't seem too usual though, as the leader of a national movement came home in her lap while his people disappeared on the western horizon headed for Dodge City. She wondered if Miss Kitty had ever been in such a predicament.

A glint of blue eyes made another appearance and the owner tried to make it linger. "Bless you, swirly-girl," he mouthed into the denim of her jeans.

Without further ceremony, Kurtis pulled him out by his scuffed shoes.

Paisley protected his head as best she could. Finding her feet, she leapt from the truck bed and ran ahead to catch the screen porch door. "Leta? We've got a sick boy." She propped the aluminum door as wide open as possible.

Kurtis made the top step about the same time the homeowner appeared in an opening of the front door jamb. Leta wiped her hands on her apron. "Goodness me, kids. Bring him right on in." The smell of baked chicken cut a greasy swath across the porch and the patient gagged.

Locking a hand through Kurtis' elbow, she halted his forward progress and motioned toward a chaise lounge out front. "Maybe outside's better—until food smells can be a friend again." She followed him across the porch. Once Kurtis deposited his load in a not-so-graceful fashion, she worked to make him as comfortable as possible.

"Sorry to skedaddle on you guys, but I've got worship team practice tonight so I have to go grab a bite to eat," her co-worker said. "Want a ride back for your car? I can drop you off."

"No, you go on Kurtis, we'll take it from here," Paisley replied.

Leta returned with a damp tea towel and handed it to her.

The aluminum door slammed as she placed the

compress across his forehead, grateful for the shade. July was making its murderous rampage across Kansas, turning wheat harvest into a real beast this year. The man's gear landed by the bushes along the curb.

Leta scurried off the porch again. "I'll go heat the hot water bottle."

The truck started up and ripped out of the yard with one motion in a gear-stripped seize of the street.

"Is this home?" the man asked.

Thoughts of him yesterday evening, standing on the makeshift platform and speaking words of fire like a young Abraham Lincoln, came to mind. She wondered how long it would take to put the spark back in those incendiary eyes, especially now that he lacked his audience.

"Yes, welcome home, Mr. Re-Occupy. This is how the rest of us are living," she added in a nonjudgmental tone. Shifting the compress to his cheekbone, she began to hum a comforting tune like her mother used to do when she had suffered earaches into the wee hours of morning.

A furrow in his brow unlatched and he snuggled deeper into the chair's padding.

Leta approached after a few minutes and held out the heated water bottle. Paisley tucked it against his ribs and lifted his left arm to keep it pinned close to his body.

"Umm. Feels good," he said, shifting the heat lower.

"I've put dinner on simmer," Leta replied. "You go get cleaned up. I think I still smell kangaroo on you."

Paisley tucked a smile into one cheek, brushing some flyaway wisps behind her ear.

Blue eyes flashed for a microsecond as the patient

concurred. "Go. I'm good."

She gave in and stood, placing a hand on Leta's shoulder. "Maybe you could ply him for a name before I go picking through his things." With a wink, she shot down the steps and pulled her uniform shirt out of her jeans in a quest to de-marsupial her exterior. She pointed out the gear pile in passing.

Leta nodded, her expression heavy with concern.

"Brace the ace," the ailing man replied, sounding more like the soapbox character from a day earlier.

Paisley halted in her tracks as she rounded the screen porch toward the back steps.

"Brace Cordan, yesterday's leader of Re-Occupy, now deposed and left for dead."

"Let's not write your obituary yet," his new guardian replied. "I'm Leta Newberry and I'm pleased to make your acquaintance. Nothing more stands between you and getting well than a gallon of my chicken noodle soup."

Paisley chuckled and excused herself from the porch's vicinity, hoping to reappear as a real member of the human race, complete with compassion and everything.

~

Good Lord above, how could a stomach hurt this bad? Brace shoved the water bottle under his shirt. Dispossession seemed to have hit him in one fell swoop after the vote last night. First he lost his office and then he lost his dinner. Respect from his peers seeped out somewhere in between, and his dissenting vote for moving on to Dodge City fell right along with his other valuables. Now they were gone, all forty-five of his tribe, following a rekindled social movement for which he'd lost heart. The water bottle burned his skin and he enjoyed the sensation.

Not that his fervor for an equal playing field had diminished, but it had been eclipsed by a need of growing personal urgency. With his first student loan payment coming due at the end of this summer, he hadn't so much as had a job offer yet. Lofty ideals didn't seem to pay the bills. Funny how his ultra-conservative father could still be right now and then. His gut had extra incentive to tighten at the predicament as he lay in a borrowed chair in some flyspeck town well beyond GPS triangulation. *There's nothing like starting from nowhere with nothing.* Oh, maybe his gear pack had been rescued, too. Make that next to nothing.

What was it that he'd prayed the night they pulled in beside that huge rock cliff outside of town? His petition had gone something like "get me off this meaningless circuit and put me someplace real." That should have left things wide open enough that an all-powerful God could arrange his exit. A disclaimer for it to be done with grace would have been a bonus looking back, as his meltdown included a humiliating electoral defeat and held a port-o-let for a wormhole of escape. The urge to gag overwhelmed him until the faint scent of lemon drifted by to quell the throaty response. Remarkable, the aroma struck him as inertly divine. He slid off without further gastric rebuke into a stationary state of sleep.

Chapter 2

Paisley walked into the director's office responding to his earlier text message. Nothing good ever came from such a beckon. She served as the unofficial second-in-command for the wildlife park, and he always managed to dump the errant task on her.

The director hovered over his computer screen like something was so compelling, he couldn't take his eyes off it.

"Hey, Marty. I'm on my way to start the feeding sessions and got your text. What's up?"

Scooting his chair to center on his guest, the man looked at her with an expression difficult to read.

She hadn't noticed the bags under his eyes before, and somehow he'd gained ten pounds since he'd been here this summer. "I'm all ears but short on time."

"Travis Donlinger left with the protest group yesterday," he said without any emotion. "When he didn't show up for work this morning, I called his house and his mother gave me the breaking news. He told her he'd be back at the end of summer."

She shifted his name plate around on the desktop. "Well, well. What do you know? I saw him hanging around a girl with a tattoo on her neck at the snow cone station Saturday, but didn't think anything of it. Looks like somebody got a bad case of wanderlust and finally had enough guts to act on it." Being hypocritical had never been her thing before, but she didn't know how to deal with the tinge of jealousy now surfacing. Good for Travis; he'd found his ticket out of here, though the stockyards of Dodge City didn't seem like much of a paradise to her.

"Who's going to handle his stations today, Paisley? Do you think Dory could handle the lorikeets by herself?" He seemed to grow more uncomfortable with the vacancy by the minute.

"How about we give Kurtis the opportunity to pick up lemur island? He's been hinting that he'd like a more hands-on station and nothing offers more contact than that place. Dory has limited skills, Marty. Don't overtax her—she's a volunteer. Her best fit would be the bunny barn. I could train her to sell the carrots and talk about the rabbits, at least until we get the new hire in place."

"What about the lorikeets, Paisley? They're good moneymakers for us and I want that aviary open for business. We have two youth groups scheduled this afternoon from Great Bend."

She bit her bottom lip trying to keep his pressure tactics at bay while she searched for resolution given her limited resources within the community. "Golly, Leta has four kiddos right now in daycare, so I don't think she could swing free and clear to cover this afternoon."A flash of blue eyes came to mind and a ray of hope clicked in place. "Uh, a long shot just came to mind, Marty. Can you give me until after lunch to get something worked out? What time are the groups coming?"

"They're sharing a bus ride out so they arrive at the same time—two o'clock."

"Okay, that gives me a little time to hook the deal and get some training done. Wow, nothing like a little pressure to keep us on our toes, right?" She turned to get her feeding schedule underway.

He smirked at her sarcasm. "See you at the grill."

The door slammed right behind her. "Maybe you won't." She broke into a trot for animal care. She wouldn't need her complimentary hot dog lunch today, as she had to go down some macaroni and cheese with the daycare kids. Plus do a little begging.

~

Two cups of chicken broth ago he landed back with his feet on the ground, and now a plate of squiggly green gelatin promised to launch him into outer orbit. Brace noted his taste buds were back on the affirmative and the roiling of his stomach long gone.

Leta appeared over the kitchen bar and gave him a sweet smile. "How are my boys doing over there?" Her gray brow arched in true concern.

Brace leveled the plate in front of his lips. "I'm coming over the topside, I think." He sniffed and the fake lime smell didn't repulse him, which he translated as permission to partake.

The boy beside him shifted his chair closer and raised his dessert plate, too. "Yeah, I'm topside like Ace," the four-year old repeated, pausing for his cue to start the slurp-fest.

Brace waited until the others had properly mimicked him, their favorite game of the morning, and thought a countdown might be in order. "Five, four, three, two, one—go." He led the troop in a gobbling exercise of enormously fun proportions. The squares of gelatin disappeared in seconds, bringing him more delight than he could express, especially since his mouth was full. Maybe he could work up to a game of chubby bunnies.

"More, please," little Cade insisted, holding his plate up like an orphan.

Leta rounded the bar with the remainder in a glass pan, pausing by each customer for the refill. "We usually try to have better manners at the lunch table." She moved around him to get the last two plates serviced.

Poised to defend his juvenile delinquent influence, Brace found himself beaten to the punch.

"Today's special 'cause we have Ace, Miss Leta," Cade explained. "We got to get him up to full speed so he can fly again. Right Ace?"

"That's right, buddy. Tomorrow we'll be better behaved, won't we?" He'd no more gotten the words out than a clatter of keys hit the bar and there stood the angel that had brought him home yesterday. Her shorts tapered down tanned thighs to well-shaped calves and ended in ballerina ankles. A uniform shirt covered a tank top underneath and hinted at curves. Maybe his once-over lingered a bit too long, as she was blushing by the time he gazed into her eyes.

A bowl of macaroni slid across the bar toward her, breaking the inertia. "You're a little late, honey," Leta said. "I thought you might not be coming today."

"Yeah, I had to take on some extra work this

morning. I'll go wash up. Be right back." She disappeared down the hall.

Brace felt a tug on his borrowed shirt sleeve.

"We gonna do this or what?" Cade demanded, his fingers itching to get at the second helping. When Leta chuckled from the kitchen, he saw the die had been cast. Maybe if he hurried the slurry, they'd be done before Paisley came back, leaving him some dignity intact. "Oh, we're going to do this all right, but just today. Then we have to save it for special occasions only."

He lifted his plate as the children readied for his count. "Five, four, three, two, one—go." He upped the plate to get the gelatin in motion. Quicker than a wink, the square disappeared and the plates plunked back down on the table. He looked up and the angel stood back at the bar, horrified at the gobbling spectacle.

"I obviously missed something coming in late." Paisley tried to drown her smile in the bowl of creamy pasta.

Leta slid a plate of apple slices toward her.

Cade wiped his mouth on the back of his hand. "Manners ain't needed if the food don't touch your teeth."

Brace brushed some crumbs off his fingertips by swiping them across the T-shirt he wore that fit two sizes too small. Maybe that's why he couldn't breathe very deep.

"If the food *doesn't* touch your teeth," Leta corrected. "I don't know if that's a proper rule or not, young man."

Paisley's smile reappeared as she gazed down at them from the bar stool.

Brace thought she somehow looked like a piece of American pie, all wholesome and at peace with her life. When she took an apple slice, a pang of something unsatisfactory pierced his chest. He cleared his throat and patted his knees, which were literally at chin height at the kids' table. Standing, he tugged his makeshift kilt in place and tried to shield himself from her reaction. On cue, the dryer buzzer went off from the back laundry room and he excused himself with a salute to his junior troops.

~

Leta broke off her gaze from the laundry area. "He's so much better already."

Paisley dug out the last noodle from her bowl and set it down in the sink. "Do you think he'd be up for outdoor work yet? We're in a tight pinch for staff this afternoon."

"His body's weak but his mind is sharp. The kids have been enjoying him all morning, and so have I." Leta's face warmed. "I'd help you myself, but I'm covered up with these four boys. It's about all I can do to keep them in line, even with a secret weapon."

Paisley could see he'd been good medicine as well as a good patient. "I might have to borrow that secret weapon after lunch, depending on how my offer goes."

Leta wrung her tea towel across the glass gelatin pan, drying its inside corners. "Go to him while you have some privacy in the laundry room." She nodded toward the children. "I can't seem to keep the kids away from him."

"Yeah, he's magnetic all right. I can see why these little metal soldiers find it hard to fight the attraction." She slipped off the stool, but didn't miss Leta's head shake at her comment. Steeling herself for the encounter, she passed by the slurp brigade and paused at the laundry room door.

Brace acknowledged her arrival with a nod and deftly covered a stack of folded boxers with the pair of shorts in his hands.

She fingered the weather stripping on the door frame. Leta always shut the sunroom off in the winter to keep the rest of her house warm, but the windows drew a nice south breeze into the house in the summertime. "First, let me say that I'm glad you're feeling better."

"Second, can I thank you for saving me last night?" he replied. "I hate to think what my ultimate deposition might have been had you not intervened." He folded a T-shirt in half, one that looked his actual size.

She sensed this would be easier than she'd originally thought. "That cleanup might have taken more than laundry soap." She decided not to tack a count onto this next comment, so he wouldn't think they had to keep score. Another shirt got folded and added to the stack. "Listen, about your plans for this afternoon."

"I have plans?" He leaned across the laundry pile. "Here lie all my worldly possessions—and now they're clean. That's the end of my to-do list, so waylay me now, I beg you."

She laughed at his unabashed coyness. She couldn't help it. When he laughed with her, his eyes sparkled like lake water. Goodness, he must be feeling better. Much better.

"Here's the thing, we're short on workers at the wildlife park. Seems Travis Donlinger took off with your Re-Occupy group and won't be back this summer."

His face reflected immediate shock.

Paisley didn't know how to read him. "I saw him chatting it up with a blond wearing a neck tattoo as they shared a snow cone Saturday. I guess she charmed him, so he's gone."

"That's Chloe. Don't expect him back, as she's been trolling for a boyfriend the whole first half of summer."

Her brow arched at the intentionality of the heart quest and a few not-so-honorable things began crisscrossing her thoughts.

"Re-Occupy is not a love-in, Paisley. I tried to hold our core values high. That doesn't mean the current leadership will keep it that way."

"Sorry for the assumption. I don't usually try to pigeonhole people. I actually Googled your resurrected movement when Marty told us you guys were coming. Who could argue with humanizing the American government? But protest isn't my thing. I'm nonconfrontational."

"Blessed are the peacemakers, right?" He leveled the sorted laundry into two equal stacks. "So how does a nonconfrontational wildlife handler go about asking for help to cover her worker shortage when she's left in a lurch?"

"Well, she finds an able-bodied person and she asks pretty please, could you step in and help us cover the lorikeets this afternoon? We have two big groups coming in at two o'clock which gives me an hour and a half for training that said someone."

"Okay, so are you officially asking me?" He touched his chest with that ridiculously tight T-shirt on.

Leta must have dredged up some of Harold's old

clothes for him while his were in the wash. Suddenly, she felt foolish standing over him in the doorway, knowing she wouldn't want someone lording position over her if the shoe was on the other foot. She stepped down into the laundry room, approached him, and cleared all else from her gaze.

He stood front and center, miraculously handsome and strangely available.

"Brace, could you come help us out? I can't cover it all, and I'm in the primate wing, half a park away from the lorikeets. I'm in a tough spot here."

He raised a finger to halt her plea and exhaled audibly. "Don't know if I'm truly able-bodied yet, and I need a paying job, not volunteer work. Could I negotiate with somebody for something more… permanent?"

Her mind swirled with the implication that he'd be staying around and she fought for an adequate reply.

Leta appeared at the doorway with her youngest charge in hand. "The crow's nest is available, Brace. Feel free to use it if you want to stay in town awhile."

Feeling the heat of indecision trickling down her neck, she reacted to his confused look by taking his hand and leading him out the back door. Leta had flanked her back walkway with a tangle of wildflowers in total disarray, but the effect came off charming nonetheless. Paisley didn't stop until they stood in front of the garage, a barn-shaped structure that had seen better days. She pointed out the tiny window centered above the double doors.

"That's what Leta calls the crow's nest, an efficiency apartment over the garage that she and Harold built for visiting missionaries and the like. I'm over there, in the upstairs apartment where the little balcony sticks out."

"We'd be neighbors, wouldn't we?" he asked, almost like the thought intrigued him.

Her discomfort ratcheted up a notch. Obviously, she hadn't thought this through far enough.

"If I could sit down while I worked, especially today, I think I could handle this."

"Gosh, I'm sorry. I probably shouldn't have dragged you outside. We should forget about this whole thing." She backtracked, way too off-balance with all the ramifications. Leading him into the shade of the garage's overhang, she tried to collect herself and think of a quick alternative plan. Nothing came to mind.

"My college degree was communications, with a minor in public relations. Like I mentioned, I think I can handle this, but it has to be a job. Take me to your leader, wildlife lady. I'll negotiate my own terms and be right there to help you with the lorikeet thing, unless you need me somewhere else."

"Okay, it's a deal. Let's start with a visit to our director, Marty Burton," she replied, suddenly buoyed by the solution. "Then you can communicate away from your perch in the aviary. I'll have Kurtis retrieve a stool out of storage. Call it an accommodation. We're ADA compliant like the big employers."

"And so goes my fortune—from the outhouse to the birdhouse. Are you sure I don't need to prove my qualifications? How about the able-bodied stipulation?" He tugged up the T-shirt's hem to better qualify himself.

She caught sight of his muscular midsection before she could cover her eyes. Making quick work of the flower-strewn path, she pulled open the back screen door and paused, thinking a word of warning might be appropriate. He literally bumped into her as she turned around, his borrowed shirt now clutched in his hand and the midday sun radiating off the bare skin of his shoulders.

"Brace listen. This is Kansas. People are modest here. We keep covered up unless we're at the water hole. Do you know what I mean?" She arched her brow in a plea.

"Hey, I'm a gymnast by training. We're used to the exposure. I'm sorry if it makes you uncomfortable."

He'd hit the nail on the head, but she wasn't about to admit it, or confess what a fine specimen of a lorikeet perch he represented. When he touched her lightly on the wrist, she knew his apology deserved a genuine response. She focused on his eyes. "You're an answer to my prayers, and don't think I'm not grateful, because I truly am. Now can you get dressed while I run upstairs? I'll take you back with me, and we'll get that training going right after you see Marty."

His face illuminated. He stuck his hand out for her to shake it. "I have a job," he quipped, giving her hand a pump.

That clarified things a bit. "Congratulations, Mr. Cordan. Welcome to Employment Central."

His eyes sparkled as he bent to claim his clean laundry as though he was relieved to be abandoning his hobo ways.

A strong sense of something positive filled her as she raced up the apartment stairs. She had the help they needed at the park and a new neighbor. A gymnast built like Fort Knox. Not that she noticed, but how could she avoid it? Science was built on the observable, after all.

And animal science remained her forte. Now, she had to merge the gymnast with the lorikeets. Both liked to soar, so the match-up stood a fighting chance. She reached for her toothbrush, ready to give the pairing a try.

Chapter 3

That's a pretty humble hourly wage, Mr. Burton," Brace commented, his eyes scanning the messy office shelves behind the park director. "Here's what I'm willing to do. I'll take that base pay starting now, plus I want an escalator clause for an increase as the weekly attendance increases. Ten percent more for me when attendance grows ten percent and right on up, calculated for the adjustment at the end of every pay period."

"I don't know," the man replied. "I've never done anything like that before."

"You're not opposed to making more money are you, Mr. Burton? I have a degree in public relations that I'll make available to you for the wildlife park. Since I share a ride over with Paisley, I'll be here an hour early every day. I can spend that time drumming up business with a focused marketing plan aimed at specific target groups."

"That sure would be handy. We've run some newspaper ads in the past."

"Which isn't enough in this day and age, is it?

Scattershot doesn't get the results you need." He splayed his fingers toward him for added drama.

The man started to sweat at the challenge. "This could end up costing me a lot."

Brace couldn't back off until he had his deal. "Only if your profits are up, and not a penny more until that happens." He sat on the edge of his seat. "Tell you what I'm willing to do. I'll add an element to your animal feeding program, an element of performing arts. I'm a gymnast and, with minimal equipment, we can give the admiring public a little show to go along with their zoo experience. That should make the day even more unforgettable and thereby draw in more crowds."

"We do have Shakespeare in the Park coming up at the end of this month," the director replied, seeming open to the possibilities. "Maybe we could work up to that with some preliminary acts, take your acrobatics, for instance, and Kurtis sings for his church. Maybe he could sing for the lemurs, too."

"There you go, a rollicking Madagascar," Brace replied in a humorous tone. "What if we tie all that up in a special package and target women's groups in a three-county area?"

"Hey, I like that a lot," Mr. Burton said. His fingers made a teepee over the desk blotter.

Brace locked his gaze on his final target. "I don't think there's any going back now, sir. We've got to do this thing and watch it take off. Your wildlife park will never be the same." When a selfish grin slid across the man's face, Brace knew he had made the sale. "Think you could put this offer in writing for me? I'll be back at closing time to sign the paperwork and we'll move on from there. Maybe we could call a staff meeting or something to launch by the end of the week."

"Good ideas, Cordan. You're like a breath of fresh air coming in here. We've been stagnant for too long."

"Fresh is always better, sir. I'm living proof of it."

"All right. Go get your training started with Paisley and I'll get the employment package together. Welcome to Tanah Keeta. I'm mighty glad you're here."

"Thank you, sir. What does the name Tanah Keeta mean anyway? It sounds Native American or something." He stood and stuck his hand out, offering the man a handshake and his best smile.

A chair shoved back as the director stood, angling a hand into his for a weak pump. "It means 'gathering place,' which is a reference to our collection of animals."

"Well, maybe your new marketing expert can extend that sentiment to infer something more," Brace replied with a wink. When he turned to exit, his thoughts shifted to Paisley. In an instant he wondered what type of performing arts she could contribute. Maybe he'd give that thought a day or so to simmer. Right now he needed to learn lorikeets, a fluttering fleet that had questionable entertainment potential.

~

Paisley extended her arms to allow the lorikeets maximum perching surface. "See how sweet they are?"

Brace mirrored her action and a couple of the bigger birds alighted on his biceps. Not ready for the clawing pinch, he winced and the birds flew up, but resettled in seconds.

Her lips pressed together as she assessed his animal handling abilities. A red blur appeared from the crown of her head and a beak started manipulating the short hairs around her part. "Is that, by any chance, the bird with the big patch of yellow?"

"Yes, it is," Brace replied. "Is he a particular fan of yours?"

The suggestive look that followed made her not want to respond, but she needed to tell him as much as possible during his hasty training session. Any tidbit of information could help him later. "That's Crackers. Way back when, he tried to fledge too early and had a rough landing. A little TLC from me got him back on his wings so he could keep pace with the others."

"Hey, I think I've been in that scenario. It's obvious these guys are used to people, so what should I concern myself with the most?"

"Well, we really need them to stay inside the enclosure, as retrieval beyond the compound can get pretty tricky. These double doors insure containment for the most part, but the larger birds can wander through the float curtain to your station out front."

"Can I shoo them back in if I get a color leak?"

She laughed at his amateur fears, took one bird off his arm, and transferred it to the fence.

He practiced by removing the other parasite and fingering it onto a bare tree limb.

"See the scoop net by the front counter there? That's your weapon of counterattack. When a bird escapes into the front space, you only have to waggle the net at them and they'll retrace their steps back into the aviary."

"So I stay up front pouring cups of food from the master brew, and trade a cup for a token as the people come through to feed the lorikeets."

"And they have a magic encounter with wildlife."

"For a token, which is how much wampum in

American dollars?"

"One token costs one dollar. You don't take real money here."

"Of course not. How silly to think I could." He made a ridiculous face that shunned the concept. He reached above her and took Crackers off her head, offering him a muscular shoulder instead. The bird took up preening his overgrown black curls.

She had to laugh. "I'm sorry. I just feel the need to go over everything once to make sure you have it down and there's no guesswork. When you work with animals, they tend to be the variable in the equation, not so much the park guests. But every now and then, there might be an act of malicious intent."

"Not on my shift. I'll be watching my flock like a hawk."

"Okay. I get your analogy, but you don't want to scare the birds, Mr. Hawk. They are safe in here and they like people to visit because people mean food. Birds have a high rate of metabolism to maintain."

"People mean food. People give token. Brace gives food cup and people share with birds. I think I have that part. Now go over closing up with me." He brushed back through the divider to the entrance atrium. Crackers flew off at the touch of the plastic curtain and he glanced back over his shoulder with a guilty look of having forgotten the bird. "Yikes, I forgot about my colorful partner."

Paisley stroked Crackers where it perched on the outer fence and brushed the other birds off with a gentle motion. She stepped through the plastic stripping with sideways ease and opened a cupboard along the back wall. "In here you have a spritz bottle, a broom, and some clean-up rags."

"Oh, great. Cleanup on aisle five," he teased as he perched on the stool.

"Sorry. Birds can't help making a mess. They can't control their excrement."

"The windshield of my old clunker could attest to that, though I always suspected they were trying to be plotting and intentional. How bad can it be, right?"

"Right. Most of it you can get with the hose's water pressure once the birds have gone to roost indoors. Go ahead and give the plants a drink while you're at it, depending on how much rain we've had."

"You mean it really does rain out here?"

She closed the cupboard and wondered how the training session had so readily turned into a comedy routine. The weatherman could answer his rhetorical question for all she cared. She had animals to attend. "You've got your water bottle, right Brace? I don't want to have to worry about you."

"I have drinking water, my emergency applesauce that Leta insisted I take, and my trusty handicap stool. If I'm going to run away, it won't be today."

She turned back toward the birds so he couldn't see that his casual comment had poked a tender spot. One last tip came to her and she beckoned him back into the aviary, grabbing a cup off the counter. Caging her other hand around it for protection, she stepped in and the birds converged on her arms. "Some smaller children are apt to spill when the birds rush to them, but something truly remarkable happens at that point." She removed the protective shield and spilled the sweet nectar across the back of her hand. Several birds moved in and began licking her skin clean, their two-toned tongues tapping the spill zone out the side of their bills.

He attempted to read the contentment on her face. "What does that feel like? Let me, let me."

She jostled some solution onto his extended palm and he immediately inherited his own mop-up crew. Crackers flew in to drink the rest out of the cup and she nosed his back feathers since both hands were taken.

"Oh, my. That's nice. Like an oil massage with Q-tips or something." He purred with pleasure.

"Be careful not to show your weak spots, Mr. Cordan. After all, we just met yesterday."

He looked up from his bird mob and the sparkle shone in his eyes. "The feel bad gave way to the feel good—and look at the bright side—I have a job." He lifted his arms slowly with a host of avian admirers on them.

That attitude would serve him well and keep her in the primate section where she belonged. She shook loose of her mob and gestured for him to carry on. "See you around five-fifteen, Brace. Enjoy your time here. It's God's little acre."

"I'm not going to run away," he replied as he dropped to one knee. He looked up at her through long black lashes that caged the blue pools behind, like the plastic curtain protected the birds.

She exited and wondered what might protect her from that magnetic gaze, as they didn't manufacture scoop nets quite that big.

~

Brace spotted another staffer approaching the lorikeet cage and tensed a bit.

"Hey, you look better," a burley fellow in uniform quipped as he passed by. "Name's Kurtis Morehead. I picked your carcass up yesterday and hauled it over to Leta's. Looks like she got you turned around with her chicken soup."

"Thanks, man. Nice to know the Good Samaritan still lives on. I'm Brace, the new lorikeet guy. Where are you headed?" A ruckus came up in the distance behind them as rowdy members of the youth group began to disperse around the park.

"I'm doing a training spot at the rhino for the next three minutes. If you've seen one rhino, you've seen them all. It typically costs five bucks for that feeding gig, but they decided to give these guys a wristband today, which gives them the option of a rhino feed or a camel ride."

"Tough decision there. Hey, Paisley didn't go over wristbands with me, are the lorikeets included in the package deal?" He pressed his face against the wire and hoped for an answer before the seasoned animal handler proceeded out of range down the sidewalk.

Kurtis backpedalled and held up a solitary finger. "One lorikeet feed per wristband. Place an 'x' on the band with the marker dangling from the string. I'll be back in a few to check on you, and then I'm on Lemur Island the rest of the day. I've been promoted."

He suspected Paisley had something to do with that which zinged his heart, a totally unexpected reaction. Deciding to get a jump on the maddening crowd, he returned to the counter and started to pour his nectar potion into a long line of cups. Once he finished the prep work, he looked up to find a customer coming through the outer door wearing a green Minecraft T-shirt. A surge of salesmanship filled his lungs.

"How about building an unforgettable experience

with a real, live bird?"

"I ran the whole way so I could be first," the boy replied, slightly out of breath.

Brace found honor in his effort, tapping the counter for the kid's wristband. He anted up with a wide grin and the marker made it official. He had his first customer. Crackers would be ecstatic.

~

A little cooperation would have gone a long way. The front gate had just closed for the day, leaving Paisley feeling the ache of being spread too thin. The mandrill had been spooked by something crossing the sky and refused to park its cotton-candy backside the entire afternoon. That put the smaller animals on alert. The golden tamarinds ended the day looking anemic. She couldn't even love on the baby Colobus monkey because its mother decided to be overprotective. The details didn't amount to anything that couldn't be smoothed over with a total lights-out. She hoped nightfall would blot out the memory of two youth groups full of hecklers from the primates' timeline. Tomorrow might be a more peaceable day, so the lion could lay down with the lamb.

Making the turn along the sculpted waterway, she glanced at Brutus and he acted famished despite catching pellets of food from the wristband gang all afternoon. She stopped long enough to snatch a pad of hay out of storage and slung it over the fence, causing the rhino to break into a trot.

"Relax, big boy. It's not like you've got any competition." She turned west to rescue her new lorikeet recruit next. As she approached, she spotted two giddy high school girls lurking outside the aviary, laughing at something Brace was saying.

"Oh, look. I'm the one with the competition," she muttered. A sudden shot of energy pulsed through her veins and she approached the cage with newfound vigor.

"Aw shucks, ladies. The main gate just closed." She glanced at her wristwatch to fan the emergency status of the flame she was trying to light. "I'll have to radio the manager to hold off on locking up, but you'd better get moving." A gasp intermixed with the last giggle and off they went, proving that gladiator sandals were not designed for speed.

"Aw shucks, ma'am," he replied through the wire as he slid back onto his stool. "I think you just saved me from the shimmery eye shadow gang. How can I ever thank you?"

"By having enough energy to walk out to my car tonight, that's how. I'm in the walking weary brigade myself." She shouldered into the aviary door and took a quick inspection of things. Everything looked neat and tidy, the concrete floor still wet from washing. "Got any tokens? I forgot to mention how to turn them in at closing." When he produced a bin that jangled as he set it on the counter, the number of tokens impressed her, as most of the afternoon crowd had been wristband. "Wow, Good work, Brace."

"You forgot to mention what to do about wristband allotments, but Kurtis came by and he gave me the skinny." He frowned melodramatically.

She stopped pocketing the tokens to address her omission. "My goof-up. We didn't get the standard orientation time, did we?"

"No, but I might suggest a checklist next time. We

could laminate it and leave it hanging in here for operational purposes."

Her eyes widened and she conceded the idea with a nod. "Did you count these?"

"Fourteen tokens, twelve birds put to roost, two disinfected hands, and one guy who needs to go by the director's office to sign his employment papers. Then we get to come back tomorrow and do it all again. Joy! Rapture!" He stood like he was posing for a statue.

Paisley recognized the scene from the classic Kansas movie. "Okay Scarecrow. I'll stop you by to see the Wizard." She hooked a finger into the knit of his T-shirt and led him out of the aviary, turning to lock the door behind them.

Unfamiliar with this part of the routine, Brace ended up a little close for comfort but didn't seem to mind the shoulder brush.

"What was it you were after in the first place? Oh yeah… a brain. Well, I hope you find one," she quipped, her mocking gaze sweeping his face.

"Actually, I always admired the Tin Man and his quest for a heart," he replied in a low voice meant only for her ears.

That sucked the wind out of her haughty sails. She mentally edited through her comebacks and none of them seemed to work. "You're a true softy then—and fully deserve the lorikeets," she admitted, lowering her pretenses. "I hope you enjoyed your afternoon."

"It was a blast, a feather-covered blast." He took a crooked step that didn't bode well.

She spied an empty catering cart behind the grill and ran to retrieve it before he crashed. He seemed to be deflating right before her eyes. "Now you're looking more like Toto running through the poppy field. Get on and I'll give you a first-class ride back to the office."

"You're too nice," he replied, scooting up on the top rack. The wheels squeaked when she shoved it forward. The momentum caused him to fall back against her. He moaned and it rippled down her shoulder through the contact.

The lean lasted and she got comfortable with it. "I have to treat my hired help right so they'll come back," she whispered into his ear.

He grinned like she had tickled him as the wheels resisted the rough concrete below.

A pang of self-consciousness slipped through her as she typically gave high regard to how things appeared. This was a different kind of day, the type you didn't overly assess. Making due always looked a little untraditional in a slapped together kind of way.

"Hired help," he repeated. "Coming back." He snuggled against her looking content, his eyes only halfway open.

If this was making due, she wondered what it would be like when he was back up to full steam. She'd worry about that later. Right now she was a weary kind of happy. *How did that happen?*

Chapter 4

Wednesday night brought the community together for a family style meal in the church's fellowship hall. Brace enjoyed the walk over beneath elm trees overhanging the road's edge. Paisley tried to speed up their pace but he hung back with intention. This would likely be their only private time and he had some things he wanted to say.

"Don't worry about not knowing anyone, I'll introduce you around," she offered. A slight smile vaulted with that reassurance as she stepped over a root hump cracking the driveway they passed. "You know Leta and Kurtis already. They'll both be there."

"What about Marty? Is he among the faithful?" He picked a stem of foxtail grass that someone missed with their weed whacker. He bowed it until the fuzzy part found her right ear.

She backhanded it away with a girlish glare. "No, Marty stays over in Great Bend while he's down here six months out of the year. HQ is in Omaha where his family lives. He claims they have six of these parks scattered around, but he never talks about the others. I think he likes to keep his professional distance, so I give him the benefit of the doubt. Small towns don't offer much appeal to outsiders."

"Depends on what you're looking for." He tickled her hand as her arms swung in rhythm with her gait. They passed a yellow train depot bearing the town's name.

She clasped the foxtail sprig reflexively, controlling his tomfoolery for the moment.

"I was praying for something more real than what I had. Look at all the 'real' around here. Real community and real people."

"Plus a real job," she added, releasing the grass sprig.

It came back to him with a dog-leg bend in the stem, making it all the more difficult to control. Watching her ponytail sway, he thought he could still get some action on her neck if he draped it just right.

She turned a corner and the church building appeared halfway up the block. The foxtail landed for a visit. She swatted the neck tickle and threshed the foxtail puff between her fingers, snuffing it out like a pest.

The playful mood that warmed his chest graduated to something more sincere as his eyes traced the church steeple skyward. He let the stem fall to the ground and grew more serious. "Paisley, you're my first friend here, and I want you to know that I appreciate all you've done for me." His throat grew tight for some reason. "I'm ready to take up residence in the crow's nest after service tonight, and hope to be the best next-door neighbor ever."

Her sideways glance deflected his sincerity, but

didn't refuse it as her pace slowed to give him an extra few moments of togetherness. "I don't know—Leta's pretty great."

He stepped sideways with his back to the church, taking her in his full field of vision. He lifted a hand to touch her but shied away when her eyes seemed to hold an ounce of fear, allowing it to skim her ponytail in innocent caress. "When I was a child, I spoke and thought like a child, but when I became a man, I put away childish things." He dropped his gaze toward the end so she wouldn't squirm under his scrutiny. "Leta's great—if you need mothering."

"I moved out of my parents' house because I didn't need smothering," she replied. Lines crinkled in the corner of her eyes and she stepped intentionally toward the church. "My mom's probably already inside, so you'll get to meet her tonight."

"And introduce me to the pastor, will you." He quick-stepped, feeling like he was trying to keep up with her. "I want to ask for prayer."

"Nobody can miss our pastor, as he's the only throwback from the NBA in the entire crowd. A real Larry Byrd, minus the hawk-beak nose, that is."

He jammed his hands into his pockets as they crossed the empty street. "Tall is good for a leader." He studied the steeple. "He doesn't have to stand on a rock to keep watch over his flock that way."

She laughed and pointed toward the rear of an add-on to the sanctuary.

"So what do you say? Can I count on your help to move into the crow's nest after this?"

She gave him a look that lacked pretense, making him wish he hadn't asked quite yet. "What are first friends for, right?" She adjusted her shirttail down over the belt loops of her jean shorts.

He tilted his head and nodded, conceding her point and allowing satisfaction to travel over his healing body.

"By the way, you probably shouldn't eat half of what's being laid out in tonight's potluck, so try to use good judgment and hold back, okay?"

"But I reserve the right to pig out unrestrained in the future."

"Duly noted, but that part is typically played by Kurtis, as you'll soon see for yourself."

"Why am I not surprised?" Suddenly, he was looking forward to some small town interaction and an occasional digestible offering.

~

Guess she'd never brought a handsome young man around for the entire village to meet, but the behind-the-back innuendo and eyebrow raising pushed Paisley to the limits of her tolerance. Thank goodness for Leta asking her to help clear the food tables off. At least her hands could have purpose even if her emotions had jumbled beneath her ribs.

"He fits right in, doesn't he?" Leta asked under her breath, ensconcing a square baking dish harshly encrusted with baked cheese.

She'd eaten from that dish but couldn't remember which vegetable representative had been layered between the dairy products. When Leta nodded to exaggerate the point, she glanced up to find Brace seated on the stage stairs engrossed in rigorous conversation with Pastor Steve. A renegade green bean threatened to sabotage her clean table, so she swiped it with her dishrag. "Some people have that knack, I suppose. It strikes me as odd that a drifter would take up here and be content with it, though. It's just little Pawnee Rock, nothing flashy or famous here."

"It's homey, that's all," Leta replied, disappearing into the corner kitchen.

She picked up the green bean dish and fell in behind her, wiping the bottom as she went. "He wants to move into the crow's nest tonight when we get home. Are you okay with that? You'll be losing a couch decoration, after all."

Leta ran the water in the sink and collected some errant crumbs in a paper towel. She made a little noise in her throat. "Are you ready for Brace to move in, honey? I like the company, but you come first in my book, and you seem a bit…uncertain…when he's around."

Paisley handed her the empty green bean dish. Soap suds soon swirled around it chased by clean, hot water. It landed right back in her hands for drying. "He's easy to like when he's sick and weak as a kitten. I saw him address the Re-Occupy group the day before they left and he was charismatic, fervent, and highly persuasive."

With one swift motion, Leta produced a tea towel from under the sink and plopped it across her palms. "Ah, and charismatic is too risky for you? Between having charm and deep blue eyes, I mean. A woman can't be too careful, right?"

She looked up at her mentor and wondered why insight came with years of experience when younger females seemed more vulnerable to mistakes. "So, yes, I'm a little off balance with a stranger possessing blue eyes and a muscular build who wants to be my friend."

Leta poked the last clean dish toward her. "He needs friends, honey. Look at him, so far away from home, and with all that debt burdening him, too."

She hastily took the green bean pan from her. "What debt, Leta? Evidently you know more of his story than I do." She placed the last dish in line with the others at the pass-through as chords of music drifted across the room. When Leta motioned her out of the kitchen so they could rejoin the others, it became clear she wouldn't have her answer any time soon. Maybe his debt stood behind the reason he'd insisted on the job, not volunteer work. She'd ask him for a clarification later, if the opportunity presented itself. Glancing toward the stage, she caught Steve finishing his prayer over Brace, his hand on his head like some kind of anointing.

"Join me if you know it," Kurtis said from a bar stool over by the upright piano. He strummed a guitar and tweaked a setting for one string, allowing Steve a polite interval of time to finish up the private prayer. He led into a worship song that boasted the power of God and his authority, allowing the church members to echo back the lines. They had finished up one round of the song before the pastor finally parted with a smile and a shoulder embrace. Steve took a seat on the front row, all too conspicuous, while Brace circled around the rows of chairs.

Leta waved a hand and flagged him down, which brought a wave in response.

Paisley's cheeks burned, but for the life of her she couldn't figure out why. She pulled a song sheet out of the Bible beneath her chair and fanned herself like she'd just eaten a hot pepper. Charisma—that was it. She was allergic to charisma all of a sudden, which gave her a reason to keep her hands off the poison ivy embodied by her new work associate. God had odd ways of working, didn't he? *Leaves of three, let them be. Eyes of blue, they won't do.*

Kurtis led into a second song as Brace landed in the metal chair beside Leta.

Great, now she had a filter to reduce her possibility for irritation. Maybe she could turn her attention to God and enjoy the midweek prayer service. Not that she wasn't grateful that Steve could focus on Brace and give him the uplifting he needed, but she needed things to be normal so she could worship God like she always had, quiet and heartfelt. Wasn't that the opposite of charismatic?

The song increased in fervor and several hands rose to give God the glory. From her peripheral vision, she saw Brace lift both his arms and hold his palms open to the sky. That guy was her lorikeet perch, increasing his surface area so more blessings could affix themselves. Her resistance to his presence peaked in a breath-squeezing wince, and then simply vanished as she allowed herself to truly mean the words she sang.

Steve's voice rippled over the group and she closed her eyes for prayer. Finally, the peace came from somewhere deep inside and radiated out so that all she sensed was Christian love all around. These were her people, the ones who knew her best and loved her worst. And amid them stood a new friend who appeared to love God like she did.

Maybe she shouldn't hold sparkly blue eyes against him. And everybody could use a little charisma now and then, right? Even little Pawnee Rock, the high place marking the midpoint of the Santa Fe Trail. When her mind lingered on the rocky promontory, she made a mental note to take Brace over for a visit as soon as he proved strong enough. Steve spoke the 'amen' and she leaned forward only to find Brace staring at her with a genuine smile that dangled under twinkling cobalt eyes.

"I somehow feel God close to us tonight," Steve said, taking his Bible in his hands. "It's like we are standing up on Pawnee Rock reaching out for him or something."

Brace sat forward as though alarmed, and shot her a quizzical glance.

We'll go," she whispered in a promise, trying to settle him back in his seat.

Leta placed a loving hand on his shoulder and gave it a maternal pat. As if to connect them, Leta reached for her next.

Paisley laced her elbow through her landlady's fragile arm to lock into the tie that binds. The pastor started talking about heaven being for real and she readily concurred. She'd already found that out.

~

Brace let Paisley in the door, hoping to show off his rearrangement of the crow's nest.

Her eyes grew wide. "Why, it looks like a blind man lives up here. How much open floor space does one person need?"

He shoved a dresser further into the perimeter. "As much as possible. These tumbling routines I'm attempting require space galore." Brace lifted the cooler Leta had sent up.

Paisley readily took it back from him. "Honestly?

Let me do the kitchen stuff. At least you can't rearrange the appliances because they're built in." She pivoted around the eat-in bar and pulled the mini-refrigerator open.

He found a footstool that matched a gold club chair and started to hoist it, but decided to do a handstand on it instead. When a gasp echoed from the kitchen, he cut it short and came back to upright.

She looked shocked. "You're breaking every rule my mother ever taught me about proper behavior inside the house."

He thought about apologizing. "I don't run with scissors." When she thawed a bit, he pressed against the bar to close the gap between them. "But I can tell—I'm too risky for you, aren't I? You always seem to be on edge, like I'm rubbing you the wrong way. That's the opposite of my intention, believe you me." He hung a guilty puppy sulk on his face to force a more compassionate response.

"I…ugh. How do I say this?" She looked a bit too flustered to be interested.

He could tell when girls were romantically interested, with their tilted heads and indirect stare-through-eyelashes coyness. Apprehension never equated to coyness, and for a second he feared hearing what she wanted to say. The moment had tailspin written all over it.

"I have…good balance," she said, centering on the balls of her feet. "I don't like to be off-balance."

His insides began to throw a party at the meek revelation. "And I make you off-balance by being here, don't I?" Off-balance was good, like a man had a chance. "Pastor Steve said in his prayer it felt like I was supposed to be here. Like God had ordained it. That's how I feel, too. Level and grounded, coming back from a stomach purge even stronger than before. And I'm working. I never could say that before."

She smiled a little, her abrasive demeanor wearing down.

He hoisted his brow like a can opener, trying to pry her loose in a favorable direction.

"I should consider myself lucky to be your first friend." She looked up and shrugged her shoulders, exhaling the angst away. "We live at two different speeds, that's all. I'm methodical and tend to hold back."

"And I'm more the gusher type, I know. But we should complement each other, right? Put us on the same team and watch out world." He toned down his gaze to medium high beam and smiled enough for her to know he was serious.

Her lips curled and two dimples popped out. "I want to take you up on Pawnee Rock tomorrow."

"Do you mean that cliff spot Pastor Steve talked about, where a person can feel closer to God?"

"Yes, it's a rock formation that lends the town its name, a pretty special place. I'm glad to be the one who gets to show it to you—but it'll be late, almost dark. I always go into Great Bend on Thursday afternoons to do Girl Scout programs at the community center. I asked Kurtis to give you a ride home after work. He said he'd invite you over to his place to grill. So I can pick you up over there when I get back, okay?"

His face twitched a little as he went through the scenario like plucking daisy petals. He had her, he had her not. And then he had her back, apparently. "Pawnee

Rock at dusk? I'd better save some energy for that escapade."

"Remember. You're on a comeback." With a salute goodbye, she headed out the door.

His head began to swirl with potential scenarios. Like any good gymnast, he threw himself vertical into a handstand, so he could see things straight. The blood rush felt almost medicinal, like he needed a good temple throb.

Chapter 5

The clouded leopard kitten had teethed on her hands so much, they'd become tender to the touch. Pawnee Rock came into view and Paisley let the thrill of showing Brace the landscape phenomenon soak through her. Only God could put such a citadel of dark Dakota sandstone in the middle of nowhere and make it mean something extraordinary. She traced the peak with her gaze and could hardly wait to get up there. Maybe she'd go straight to Kurtis' house and let Brace see her kitty since the leopards weren't out on public display. Marty wanted to sell these twins, but she hadn't put much stock in his idle threat.

She passed the wildlife park and turned right on the next residential road, pulling in front of the second house. The smell of beef being grilled wafted across the breeze. She lifted the animal carrier out of the back seat and walked along the unpaved driveway. Sounds of merriment filtered from the backyard and she knew she'd arrived too early, even though the house shadows were lengthy across the front yard. The leopard meowed at the commotion, accentuated by the smell of meat, so she cradled the carrier in both hands. They'd had a good afternoon together, despite the nibbling teeth.

"Hey, Paisley's back." Kurtis launched a football toward the garage. Intentionally impossible to reach, the pass deflected off the roof. When Brace scrambled under it with a diving catch, Kurtis clapped with approval.

She shoved the carrier onto the picnic table bench. "Looks like you guys are having fun." A bag of chips gaped open so she stole a handful. The kitty called again.

"Wow, who's this?" Brace tucked the ball into his elbow and bent to eye the critter through the cage door. A warning spit shot back at him.

"This is Cirrus, our clouded leopard kitten. She has a twin sister, Cumulus." Motioning him back, she lowered the door and coaxed the wildcat out.

"Lose the ball under the table." Kurtis gestured for the bundle of cat-fuzz arched in her grip. Brace made a stealth move and shouldered up against her gentle assistant animal handler.

She made the transfer and the kitten calmed down with his familiar touch, kneading his bulging stomach with its oversized paws.

Brace stood spellbound by the junior feline. "How awesome is this?" He extended a brave finger toward its head, landing his stroke right between two gray-blue eyes. When he repeated the action, the kitten started purring. "Only in Pawnee Rock could something this raise-the-roof be happening in somebody's backyard."

She eyed the grill. "Got enough burgers to share?

The Girl Scouts were making their own pizzas for dinner, so I begged off."

Brace stuck out his tongue and the leopard did the same.

The coincidence seemed noteworthy. She turned her attention to the badminton net by the mulberry tree. "Looks like your berries will be ripe by next week. Bring Leta some and she'll bake you a cobbler or something."

"Plenty of burgers," Kurtis replied, "but I'd better check on 'em." He ditched the kitten into Brace's arms.

He tried to cast his spell over the feline. Scrunching his eyes closed, he stuck out his tongue again and the cat mimicked him like before.

She rescued the air-scratching back legs and tucked the lanky critter fully onto his forearm. "I think Cirrus likes you. Maybe you could develop an act together if Marty doesn't sell her off beforehand."

Brace froze to protest the selling option, shaking his head in refusal.

"We've had good fortune in getting this rare species to breed. The offspring bring a good price, so Marty sells off the litter to keep the rest fed during winter."

"Maybe after my plan is implemented, we won't have to resort to selling our stock." He buried his nose in the cat's fur. The purr translated into a warning threat from the cat's throat.

Paisley rescued the last few morsels of cat food from her pocket and let it nibble them from her hand.

From such close range, Brace stared at the rough conditions of her hands. A wave of concern swept over his countenance. "Let's put the kitty back in and get you cleaned up." He lowered the animal level with the door.

She tucked its head low and helped him place her inside, flipping up the door before the animal could protest.

Brace pulled at her elbow and led the way to a faucet off the back steps. A bar of soap dangled from a netting bag, and he pushed it toward her.

She stuck her hands under the thin fluid stream. "So what's this plan you're going to implement and save the wildlife park from financial ruin?"

He gave a furtive glance back toward Kurtis at the grill and returned his focus on her at the faucet, giving a slight wink. "Let's save it for our cliff explore later tonight."

Something about the coziness in his voice made it sound like the proper thing to do. She looked forward to it even.

"Right now we've got to fend off cat scratch fever and get you something cleaner to eat than Scout-mauled pizza." He took her by the wrist and led her back to the table where he dabbed at her hands with a paper napkin. "Sit. Stay," he commanded, pointing a threatening finger in her face.

She froze in submission as he backed away toward Kurtis at the grill. How nice to be fussed over. She scanned the familiar backyard. The kitten pawed at her through the wire mesh of the cage door, but she sat a little too far out of reach, like under-ripe mulberries.

~

Gasoline-tinted skies rimmed the massive rock as Brace approached the landmark up-close for the first time. Buoyed by walking alone with Paisley at the close of day, he wasn't about to let a little fatigue stymie the opportunity. They followed the entrance road that wound around the base of the hill, making him search for a shortcut. All he found was sheer rock face.

He pointed toward a rough cut in the slope. "Amazing formation." Darker than the sky beyond, the deep stain that bled through the rock seemed appropriate for some reason. "Any history of suffering here? The rock seems dark to me."

"Yeah. It's history includes suffering and the taint of plotting against fellow man. Like many things, the advantage of a lookout post can lend itself to good or bad, depending on the motivation of the person standing there. From up top, you can see into three counties at once."

"And I'm guessing that includes quite a length of the Santa Fe Trail, right?" Try as he might, he couldn't keep from puffing between words. He wondered if the air was thinner up here, but they hadn't even gotten beyond the base yet, so that couldn't be it. The burger sat like a rock in his gut, making it impossible to draw a deep breath. The slowness of his digestive recovery irked him.

"You're winded, so let's slow down a bit," she replied, falling a half-step back.

He caught sight of several kids racing bikes down the hill, rounding the curve, and flying like the wind. It struck him as carefree movement from high to low.

Paisley put her arms out and made them brake as they approached. "Hey there, Jacey. How's the view tonight?"

"Getting dark up there, Paisley. You guys better hurry up," the girl replied.

"Say, could we borrow your bike for the trip up? My

friend Brace is running out of steam here. He's been sick, but Miss Leta's nursing him back to full strength."

"Not there yet, huh?" she said, giving him the once-over. Her left leg flipped across the seat as she stood and surrendered the bicycle.

He stood stock-still, utterly amazed. Reminded to reconsider small town values, he held the handlebar and saluted her selfless action. The girl situated on the front bar of her friend's bike while Paisley slid onto the seat of the surrendered vehicle, leaving him without a perch.

"Thanks a bunch, Jacey. I'll tuck it on your front porch when we come back in," Paisley said. The kids pedaled off toward home.

Brace assessed his options—a back tow plank and the not-so-comfy looking cradle of the handle bars.

"Sit up front so you can see the hill as we ascend."

"Does that offer come with any padding?" he joked. He stepped behind her to straddle the back wheel to ride the tow plank. Before he could hoist into position, she had his accommodation in place, her uniform shirt. Intrigued, he walked by her, threw his frame onto the handlebars, and shifted to get his weight centered. "Forward ho," he called, pointing up to the rock pinnacle. When she threw her weight on the pedal, he lurched with the momentum. At least he'd forgotten about his stomach ache, as he had other body parts reporting in right now while the chrome handlebars became his newest acquaintance.

"I'll pedal as far as I can, then I'll push you up the rest of the way. Someday soon you'll be back to full strength, so let's enjoy this novelty while we can." A crack in the road pavement accentuated her statement.

His teeth slammed together with the jarring. It might

be a good thing novelty was short-lived by definition, as he hated playing the part of the weakling. Paisley made an outstanding heroine, though, pretty and sensitive all at the same time. "What's that rocket shape up there?" He squinted into the apricot sky capping the rocky peak.

The trail steepened and she stood to get more oomph on the pedal. "Obelisk for the historical marker," she replied. Within ten yards, all forward motion ceased.

He jumped clear of the front wheel and landed in a crouch.

"Get on and I'll push you up. I didn't get my run in today, so this can take its place."

"Should I just park all my male pride back here or what?" He stepped uphill in desertion.

Paisley lowered the kickstand to abandon the bike.

The slope pulled at the back of his calves and he thought of the workout potential of the anomaly. Not too much uphill around here except for a treadmill setting. Once he got his stamina back, he could train here to maintain his fitness, which he would need as a gymnast if his master plan worked.

She soon passed him. "Don't make me have to pull you up behind me, as my hands still hurt from Cirrus."

"No touch zone," he replied, instantly saddened at the prohibition. Maybe that was God's way of working all things together for his good. Right now, the only touch he need was stomach-deep. He hoped the Great Physician held office hours atop giant rock formations tonight.

Though drained at making the pinnacle, the view came as an immediate reward. With his back to the obelisk, Brace turned and searched the horizon in every direction.

Paisley wandered into the rock pavilion and soon waved to him from its flat roof.

Exhaustion tugged at his legs but he fought the weakness, buoyed by proximity to the Most High and mesmerized by the scenic earth beyond. Tranquility seeped through him as he started to pray. He kept his eyes open so as not to desecrate the honor of the overlook. In the distance, car headlights pulsed down the highway blending into a rope-light decoration that festooned the perpetual plains.

His prayer soon turned audible. "This place is real, resplendently real, Heavenly Father. Thank you for slowing my sprint across the face of your green earth so I could see this, have this moment. I claim your healing here, from my sick, indebted self to who you want me to be. I relinquish all to your will. Amen." Movement caught his eye atop the pavilion and the copper-streaked sky became a backdrop for a free-spirited dancer, with only the wind and a recovering aerialist as witnesses. Mesmerizing visuals seeped deeper into his chest until the first pang of longing birthed under his ribs. When she stopped dancing, a strong urge to explore the pavilion overtook his senses.

"A pinnacle with a self-imposed no touch zone," he repeated, finding the sidewalk entry for the rock structure. A rectangular atrium opened before him, its ceiling blocking his view of the ever-changing evening sky. When a spiraling iron helix appeared in the corner, he ran to it and took the stairs two at a time. He found her sitting in the far corner, acting as though nothing had happened.

Approaching, he framed the image of her silhouette

against the sky and took a mind picture that seemed to quell the longing. "Nice breeze up here," he said. "Can I sit with you?"

She motioned to the rock ledge at right angles to her seat.

In a blink, he was laid out on the still-warm rock. When he could count twenty star-pricks in the night sky, the need for conversation tugged at him.

"Want to hear my plan for the wildlife park?" he asked, lifting his head to face her.

She shifted from the corner and took his head in her lap, her fingertips barely touching him.

It struck him like angel's breath. His involuntary breach of the no touch zone made him hesitant to exhale, lest he somehow jeopardize his position and be penalized for it. No judgment came though, only her left hand which alighted at the base of his throat along the ribbed neckline of his T-shirt. His mind raced, wondering if he should share the gist of it and let the night fall magically quiet between them.

She stroked through his hair with the fingers of her right hand. "Tell me all your hopes and dreams," she replied in a wind-swept voice.

He closed his eyes. Only the night breeze and her touch influenced his thoughts. "My dream is to add an element of performance to the animal acts in the park. I hope you'll support me in my quest to accomplish it. I'm pitching the idea to the whole crew in the morning at staff meeting, so maybe you can make some suggestions to help me avoid a few potholes along the way. We have to be all in, one hundred percent for the whole team, as though called by God to do this good work."

"Your being here is a real God thing, Brace. If he's calling us to do more or to be more, then we have to listen like we're on the verge of obeying already."

Her receptivity outright slayed him. "Wow, and I thought I was going to have to win you over, swirly-girl." Relief eased his next breath.

Her fingers traced a long caress from the front of his hairline back over the crown of his head. She dusted a few hairs back into place and picked a new spot to fuss over.

His insides melted under each stroke of her touch. His power of persuasion seemed to flit like a badminton birdie over the net, which would have made him uncomfortable under normal circumstances. But he was in the realm of small-town-real, an unnatural microcosm with a satisfying fit. How had it taken him so long to get here? The sky darkened to an intense hue he'd never seen before. The color wheel had a new wedge, and he admired it.

~

From the height of the moon Paisley knew midnight approached, and though she would rue this late night encounter in the morning, she could barely pull away from it in the moment. Brace stirred and shifted his head in her lap, so she separated in increments, moving her left hand off his collarbone. Similarly, his master plan would shift her private rooftop dance to the highly visible main stage of multiple animal enclosures, forcing her to dig deep to find the courage to step out. While graceful movement came like a gift from God, the stage had always struck her as a vaudeville platform for hawking one's wares. It wasn't the place for her.

Fear wasn't the right word, it seemed more like

loathing. Maybe the animals would lend her some comfort, as they shared the stage in their unpredictability. If she could focus her attention on the animals, maybe the dance would unravel in a more natural sequence, like a ripple on the pond. She wasn't the rock in the center of the splash, but she could be a ripple.

Brace awakened and lifted his head. "Guess we'd better get back before Leta has the law out looking for us," he joked, wiping a hand across his face to sober up for the descent. He stood and led the way back to the stairs.

She followed, even though her heart still longed for something more. Their separation soon gave her the chills.

Brace started down the spiral stairs backward, his face tilted toward the night sky.

She stepped down through the first twist to find him waiting halfway down. Why he had held up? With the lighting impossible at ceiling level down below, she had to default to her other senses as her hands gripped the rail. She heard his breath draw and then felt the matching exhale on the bare skin of her shoulder as he shifted up to the step she occupied.

"I'm not going to forget this night any time soon," he whispered, too close for comfort. His hug came strong of arm like a rising tide, uninhibited by the moon's pull. It held for a generous duration.

Her heart grew content inside her weary frame. Now both of them wouldn't forget this night, as affection rippled out from the rock pinnacle over the prairie. She nestled her forehead into the crook of his neck, afraid he might try to kiss her, and even more fearful that she'd let him. When he carried her down the rest of the stairway, she floated the rest of the way home in every sense of the word.

Chapter 6

A tactical error, he'd stepped in front of his audience without knowing a majority of the individuals involved. Allowing his gaze to skim the group, Brace counted eleven people, three of whom he knew. If things came down to a vote today, his lack of preparedness would riddle him like a shot in the foot. He should have hobnobbed with the guy manning the grill yesterday when he held a hot dog's sway over him. Guess it was too late to add condiments now.

"I appreciate Marty calling this staff meeting for my benefit. For those who haven't met me yet, I'm Brace Cordan, mastermind of the lorikeet enclosure."

Kurtis snickered to help him break the ice as Marty started circumnavigating the tight space, handing out envelopes.

"We're just here for our paychecks," said the guy who ran the camel rides. He held his hand out and Marty slapped an envelope into his palm.

The director nodded to him as a go-ahead, but he knew it would be bad form to rush it. "You guys have the perfect backdrop for something special here at

Tanah Keeta. Kudos for that, as the work it took to get us this far is apparent, even to my untrained eye." He ended his comment with a meaningful glance at Paisley.

She fanned an envelope under her chin and hitched her brow in response.

"What I'm going to pose to you today is that we kick things up a notch to work on increasing attendance. We won't have to build one new building or acquire another critter in the process. In fact, what I think you already have the perfect venue in place for is performance—by us with our animals in the act."

He continued, trying to build momentum. "What would it feel like if we doubled our attendance? Amazing, right? Much more attention for the animals, more funding for their food, and more creative stimulation for the staff. The list of benefits goes on and on. We'd sell more tokens, more hot dogs at the grill, and more kitschy souvenirs in the gift shop."

"Hold on, Brace," Kurtis said. "You're about to make Marty so happy, he has to smile. I'm not sure we can handle that level of change around here." Laughter rolled across the room and the director played Grinch by using two fingers to force the corners of his mouth up.

"Okay, now the gauntlet has really been thrown down," Brace replied. "Here's my preliminary idea to accomplish this boost in attendance. We have to figure out what kinds of acts we can reasonably add, you know, assess our talent base. Then I'm going to work up a marketing plan that targets our outreach for the greatest level of success. We'll pitch it to a three-county area, and see if we can get the buses rolling into our parking lot."

"Plenty of parking capacity out there," Kurtis replied. "Count me in for a singing act. I could sing to the lemurs and they'd be all over me. Maybe like a Madagascar fun frolic."

"Love the idea, absolutely love it," he responded with enthusiasm. He couldn't have planted that comment and been in better shape. "I'm a gymnast and I'd like to try an aerial act with the lorikeets. It would be flashy color and high movement at the same time. Anybody else?"

"I'll dance in the primate wing," Paisley replied. "I think I could get the Colobus monkeys in motion and maybe the Schmidt's and DeBrazza's Guenon. Especially if I held their babies like a dance partner."

A touch of jealousy struck beneath his sternum, but Brace couldn't afford to lose focus now. His eyes searched for the next volunteer.

"Hey," Kurtis added. "I could play some classical guitar in the background for Paisley if we could sequence the timing of the shows to allow for helping one another out."

"Excellent point, my friend. I'll work that around on paper and see where it leads. We could do a progressive show and lead the crowd through it, maybe once in the morning and once in the afternoon. That leaves plenty of time for wandering the premises to feed the animals."

"Travis played the harmonica better than anybody I ever heard," the guy from the grill commented. "Maybe we can get him to come back."

Brace had to think fast or this would take off into the realm of "what if" and lose the focus of reality fast as a wink. "Strong point, grill-master," he conceded. "We have to start with our current staff, but if we're successful, we can expand. Travis will be back by summer's end so let's hope we're ready for him. This can benefit the entire community, if we do it right."

"I'd like to try comedy with an animal act," the camel tamer said. "Maybe it could combine some animals that don't get much exposure, like the alpacas and the tortoises from the petting zoo. We could reposition the amphitheater seats to focus on the corral."

Brace deferred to Paisley for her expertise and she shot a thumbs-up into the air. He clapped and then thought he'd better test the waters. "Hit me with something funny, whatever your name is."

"It's Edgar. Okay, here goes. Have you ever wondered why it's so hard to get something over on the tortoises?" He stood and shrugged his shoulders.

Brace shook his head and held his palm out for the delivery.

"Because, they've been playing the shell game successfully all their lives."

"Ba-dum-bum," Kurtis added, drumming the manager's desk beside him. The girl that operated the front gate window laughed and tried to cover her mouth. Her eyes shone with admiration for the funny guy, and he sat down enjoying an ounce more validation that he'd had before.

Brace pointed at her like she had fallen into the spotlight. "You're about to become very busy, young lady. Want to throw in with the performers at all?"

She squirmed a bit but finally found something to suggest. "My name's Cerise and I'm pretty good at memorizing. I usually lend myself to a soliloquy or two at our Shakespeare Festival. That's more like dramatic reading, I guess. It could be fun with a giraffe peeking over my head."

"Or in the kangaroo village," Edgar said. Their eyes met and she thanked him in a personal way.

Brace cleared his throat as Marty tapped his watch. "Let me get this worked into a plan," he replied, moving forward without the consensus vote. "With the traditional Shakespeare in the Park on our immediate horizon, I'm thinking maybe we should…"

"Fuse the two together," Paisley added. "We can still hold some of the traditional programs from the works of Shakespeare, both comedic and tragic, while adding performance elements that are contemporary. That way, we'll have a guaranteed audience and can build on our success from there. It's only three weeks away, so our options are limited."

"As is our practice time," Brace said. "Think about this over the weekend and let's meet again Monday. I'll have a rough draft of a schedule outlined and we'll fill in the acts you bring to the table. Once I know what to expect, I can write the marketing copy and get the word out to the three-county area."

"Make that Tuesday, not Monday, as I'm sure everyone wants their day off left intact," Marty said, attempting to ride Brace's wave of energy. Out of character, his enthusiasm fell flat as everyone got up to adjourn the meeting. "Okay team, now get out there and land some tokens today."

"Together we can do this," Brace called, raising his hand as if to invoke a blessing. Kurtis turned it into a high five and slapped his palm, so he offered his other hand to Paisley.

She put a tentative hand in his and he grabbed it.

"Would you rather have this?" Marty teased, waving an envelope with his name on it. "Pay for one week only—but it's better than nothing."

Brace opted to keep her hand but relinquished the other, crossing arms to get his first paycheck. "And so ends a long line of nothing," he said in a melodramatic voice. Kurtis clapped and the impulse to soar swept over him as he tucked the pay into his back pocket.

"Check his math," Paisley warned under her breath. She stepped past him and her eyes spoke something else. "Quitting time is four o'clock today so we can all run to Great Bend for the bank."

"Take me with you," he replied. The wink spilled out like a bonus that she didn't seem to mind. His head started spinning at the thought of making a deposit. He'd need to set up an account, of course, but accrual had to start somewhere. Lucky for him, it started today.

~

Her day-off adventure had taken a circuitous twist when Leta's youngest charge proved too sick to hit the road, so participation had dropped off to the two of them. Brace literally hovered out of her car window studying everything they passed beyond Great Bend. Ellinwood wasn't far down the road but it stood deep in unusual history. She had mentioned the underground cowboy lair once and Brace had been like a kid ever since. His stamina had come back by the week's end, and with it came immense curiosity. Next time, she'd wait until after church service to mention any possible adventures.

The main intersection of the town appeared up

ahead. She slowed the car and started searching for a parking spot amid faded brick buildings that rose from the prairie like specters. The neon sign in the antique store's window blinked "open," so she breathed a sigh of relief and motioned toward the edifice. He shot out of the passenger side and glided up the ancient steps in three strides, leaving her to place the sunscreen across the windshield by herself. Stepping up to the old building, she allowed the adventure to begin. A historic bronze plaque read "Wolf Hotel: 1894" which impressed her, though the wooden "haunted" sign beneath did not.

~

Brace crossed the street and approached the Dick Building along its historic loading ramp behind the store. Only a set of storm cellar doors reinforced with wrought iron bars stood between him and a true cowboy adventure. The tour guide jangled his keys and a Mennonite family stood aside to allow him access. Paisley stood by a planter of lavender flowers admiring the busy work of two bumble bees. German immigrants may have excavated these underground rooms, but what remained would be at the mercy of a group of humble Midwestern folk today.

The doors banged open and the guide stated his welcome to the world of a cowboy which was all the invitation Brace needed. With spry steps, he launched his attack, pulling Paisley down into the dark corridor with him ahead of the group. The passageway smelled of dry dust and musty leather. He touched the rock walls flanking the entranceway and brought Paisley up beside him. They passed a weak light bulb that had been added as a modern convenience for the tourist trade. The room opened up around them in a long rectangle.

Contraptions of every sort crowded the room with work tables and cobblers benches fit like aprons along the stone and plaster walls. Leather goods harkening to various types of rigs draped the walls, and a string-tied cover for the back of a mule hung like a quilt from the rafters. Their guide introduced the harness room and talked about what had been left behind in the underground world after the residents had decided to fill in most of the rooms. After being encouraged to try the primitive machinery, he felt compelled to touch each one.

As they narrowed down a corridor to the next stop, a door to the coal bins had been left open for the group to enjoy the sunlight filtering down through the removable plank sidewalk where Old West manhole covers made of transparent mica cast a pinkish light. Brace stepped in trying to imagine a man shoveling coal to shove back the cold of winter. When Paisley appeared under the pink shaft of light, his study shifted to her, smooth and surreal like a marble statue. The impulse to touch her came and went as the guide called for them to enter the next room.

Next, a wallpapered room had been made brighter with additional light bulbs, catching his fancy with its authentic attitude. Jung's Barbershop had it all—manly tools for shaving, bullet holes embedded in the plaster walls, and an awesome red leather chair where the barber plied his trade. The call for a volunteer went up and he quickly sat in the barber's chair, ready for service. Goodness knows he could use a haircut. Their leader wheeled him around and he glimpsed Paisley's delight at his predicament in an angled plate glass mirror that must have been a hundred years old. A chide came next for his neglect of oral hygiene, and the stand-in barber pretended to extract an abscessed tooth. When a camera flashed, he knew he'd been captured in a cowboy moment. Too bad they hadn't offered a shave and a haircut for two bits.

After a brief wander around the barbershop hangout, he moved the red checkers into a strategic ambush and followed the group into the last room, the bath and laundry. Amid the tubs and washboards, the wringer dryer for the denim jeans, the clotheslines, drying racks, and iron collection stood twin tin bathtubs, wide at the head end and tapered at the feet. At the end of his spiel, the guide invited photos, so he shot Paisley a dare-you glance. She handed her camera to a young farm hand and gave him a few instructions. He nestled down into his tub and watched as she tried to get in the next tub gracefully. Right before the picture clicked, he reached for her arm and she tried to shove his hand away playfully, laughing at his attack.

A partial wall hid what looked like the furnishings for a hotel room. An old wrought iron bed sat tucked in the nook with a traveler's trunk beside it, bound with leather straps. Stroking his mustache, the guide mentioned how long it took jeans to dry and stated the cowboys could get another specialty service while here. As soon as the term "soiled doves" came out of the man's mouth, Brace clamped his hands over Paisley's ears and swallowed to keep his objection from blurting out. The Mennonite family looked aghast at the insinuation, as the cowboy's world began to lose a little of its luster. When the tour guide revealed that no other women would have passed through the underground doors back in the day, he secretly wished he could have spared Paisley the innuendo of immoral services, especially in the cleanup room.

With the tour over, he stumbled up the same storm cellar stairs and had to shield his eyes from the direct afternoon sun. He stepped in and out of a time warp, yet one truth stood out in his mind. No matter how industrious or ingenious mankind could be, the heart was deceitful and desperately wicked, not to be trusted without an infusion of the Almighty. He saw a steeple in the distance and begged God to ride with him down the trail, just like any cowboy would have. Idle hands were the devil's workshop, and now he could add long-drying jeans to the naughty list. Good thing his shorts were quick-drying twill. Plus his hands had more than they could do to prepare performances for the festival at Tanah Keeta.

Paisley smiled at him from the lavender planter, seeming to have enjoyed the underground tour.

A promise he'd made to himself resurfaced. As long as the student loan hung over his head, he was not a free man—so his heart couldn't be free either. He'd call his father tonight, ask him to bring out the gymnastic equipment from their garage, and hand-deliver his loan payment packet. Time had come for him to step out of the cowboy wash tub and man up as a responsible citizen, one who could be vested in the local community, not a mere passer-through.

Chapter 7

Following a brain trust session in Leta's sunroom Monday night, Tuesday dawned with a performance roster full of blank lines for writing in acts and a suggested rotation between areas of the park. Paisley respected Brace's efforts to keep the randomness contained because special events took a touch of finesse to pull off. She typically ran herself ragged in the process, because Marty was full of suggestions, but lacked follow-through. Somehow he always managed to carry off the role looking successful while investing little energy to get there. Fortunately, for the festival's sake, the blanks had largely filled in with willing amateur performers earlier in a staff meeting. When Brace made a point of meeting everyone in the room, the effort fed into her growing admiration of him.

She mixed the food trays together and sealed them in plastic tubs for ease of transporting around the park. Some of the feed bags were depleting, so she'd have to speak to Marty about it. He'd always insisted on being in charge of procurement, so he could track expenses.

Maybe she should start begging produce from the west-side grocery store in Great Bend. Too bad she hadn't thought of that after her run to the bank on Friday. Maybe Brace would help her. She'd mention it to him tonight and get his feedback.

The plastic pitcher for the lorikeet enclosure caught her eye, so she addressed that assignment next. Pulling an unopened jar of applesauce from the cabinet overhead, she popped the lid and poured in half the contents. Next, she pulled a protein packet from the far drawer and ripped the foil open to dump in the powder. Lowering the pitcher under the faucet, she filled it three-quarters full of water and watched the milky green formula come to the desired consistency. She added a touch of sucrose and stirred the sweetener into solution, capping the pitcher for delivery.

Anticipation bloomed as she placed the lorikeet food on the cart. The pitcher guaranteed her a little more time with Brace this morning. Her motivation usually came from time spent with the various animals, so having the human attraction was new to her, though equally alluring. She'd stopped trying to keep her mind off of him after their visit to Pawnee Rock. Brace, with his sparkling blue eyes and gentlemanly ways, was a force to be reckoned with—not ignored. She told herself that the magnetism between them came with being friends first, but she hadn't expected it to grow. And he had been spending a great deal of time with her.

A tiny voice in the back of her head cautioned her not to read too much into her new friend and his captivating attention. A small-town girl with mousy brown hair tending animals in a wildlife park wouldn't amount to much in the eyes of a national leader, even one that had fallen off the gypsy wagon of disillusionment. She'd play it cautious and hide behind her festival performance with the busyness it would generate. Maybe that would give her the time she needed to separate the real from the imaginary. She backed into the push bar and opened the door, pulling the food cart behind her. Animals were easier, she realized with a sigh.

~

With the food cart due to arrive, Brace thought he had a few minutes to follow up on a nagging worry that had plagued him since he'd awakened. His strength seemed to be arriving back in increments when he needed it in full measure. He brought the stool out into the aviary with the hope of trying to plank for a test of his abdominal muscles. Upper body strength proved to be another matter entirely, as his attempted pull-ups on Leta's clothesline pole quickly attested. Crackers flew at his head and he ducked.

Somehow he stubbed his toe on the stool leg with his next step, causing his body to lurch forward. Unable to balance the stool any longer, he started to go down right on top of it in a linebacker's tackle. Spreading his knuckles clear just before contact with the concrete, his chest took the brunt of the impact, knocking the wind out of him. The scene unfolded from there on the tips of red wings, as the birds startled at the commotion, and then they miraculously came to his aid. Before he could push off the stool and recover, the birds had covered his horizontal self from head to feet. He had become a bird platform.

Hesitant at what to do next, he drew a breath and tried to collect his thoughts. Several of the lorikeets shifted positions on his back as he felt the claw-pinch through his shirt. One bird found his overgrown locks and started grooming his hair. He bowed his head and the bird climbed onto it for a higher perch. The nibble at his ear gave him goose bumps. What a predicament he'd fallen into.

"Crackers baby, what ya doing?" a female voice asked in candy sweetness.

He heard the plastic curtain part and knew he had human company now—and maybe a helping hand up.

"Brace, play along and stay down there a minute."

He hadn't even heard the food cart but Paisley was there now assessing the situation. She sounded mysterious, like she'd seen something out of the ordinary. Too bad all he could see was concrete. And his ribs hurt.

"Were you trying to have them come to you, Brace, or was it a happenstance?"

"Back where I'm from, we call this an accident. I stumbled with the stool and fell. The birds were onto me in a matter of moments. I had the wind knocked out of me, so getting up right away wasn't an option. I'm fine now. Thanks for your obvious concern."

"I'm intrigued by their response, as the typical avian reaction would be to fly away from the sudden movement. This is unnatural, like you have favor or something. Maybe with a little training, your aerial act could incorporate this flocking phenomenon."

"Wow, I like that idea a lot. Would I have to be horizontal? That takes a whole different set of muscles." He groaned while Crackers manifested its domain across his head.

She laughed at him. Then her fingers stroked his

forearm and the favor took on a new dimension. "Think you can stand up now? I'd like to see if we can simulate their response by having you assume another pose, one you might use in your gymnastics act."

"Well, I actually came in here to attempt a plank across the stool but my ribs are so tender from impact, I may not be able to pull it off." He pushed off the ground with a grunt.

Paisley helped draw him into a standing position while the lorikeets flew off in random directions. "Come out here and let me look at you." She pulled him back through the curtain divider.

He followed her out of the aviary and lifted his shirttail. Sunlight revealed a six-inch streak of red skin across the middle of his chest.

She reached into a soft-side cooler and borrowed a gel pack, tucking it against his ribs. "It could be a one-time incidence, never to be repeated."

"What, you taking care of me?" His grin grew when she squirmed.

"No, the birds, you… you…"

"Aerialist," he said with a slight bow.

"Okay, Brace, the avian aerialist." She folded her arms like she had grown impatient. Her liquid brown eyes seemed content to focus on him.

Maybe he should try to repeat the trick while she was his audience-of-one. "Let's go ahead and give it a shot. You've got other deliveries to make and don't need to be wasting time gawking at little old me." He gestured toward the door.

She shook her head in refusal. She held up a finger to indicate 'one' and pointed inside.

He saluted, pleasured to be the sole object of her

attention. Through the curtain he could see that the stool had been left at an odd angle. He could scoop it up, center it under his hips and stiffen into the plank, all in one fluid motion. Once the perch had been set up, the birds would be free to come alight. Since he could only control so much, he found himself uttering a prayer for God's assistance as he stepped sideways through the curtain. In his peripheral vision, Paisley moved to the corner of the enclosure, mostly hidden but able to observe. Here went nothing—and everything at the same time.

His plank move fell into place seamlessly and it soon felt like flying atop the stool. Typically, the Re-Occupy crowd would be applauding by now, but he liked this scenario even more as the sound of bird wings swished the air. Within seconds, all twelve birds had landed on his horizontal perch, making him attempt to hold the pose through an eternity of muscular contraction. When he knew the leaden feeling in his legs would ultimately corrupt the pose, he lowered them as part of the routine, staying bent at the waist as he stood. Slowly, he opened the angle of his stance until the birds slumped and eventually had to take wing. He faced the wire mesh of the outer wall and waited for her to come to him.

Paisley stepped up and interlocked her fingers through the mesh. "God has surely given you this gift, Brace," she whispered, making brief eye contact but unwilling to hold it.

He touched her fingers by interlacing his through the caging, needing to connect. "Every good gift is from above," he quoted. "Wish I could express how remarkable it feels."

"This will come across like pure magic on the stage,

but we'll always recognize it as the favor of God, unspoken between us." She gazed up with sincerity and held it.

"Unspoken," he repeated, swallowing down the emotion threatening to escape. Crackers flew over, alighting on his shoulder.

"I suppose you want your magic potion, pretty bird," she said, the candy voice returning as she drew away.

His smile hunkered into one cheek as he wondered how nice her candy voice might feel wooing him instead. It made him tingle a little to even consider it.

~

"Good golly, the flies are bad today," Paisley said, as she downed the last bite of her hot dog. Her friend looked up from wiping the condiment pumps and waved away a swarm of flying germ-carriers. "Oh, here comes Brace. Could you get his lunch ready, Amyl? I want to take him over to Lemur Island and let Kurtis run through his music with us." The slender man wrapped the trashcan liner into a knot and gave her a wave, carting off half the local fly population inside the bag.

"Hey there," Brace called. "Shoot me with a special, Amyl."

"Coming right up, birdman," the grill-master replied. The sounds of water flowing reassured her that quality control was being practiced, at least in the food prep area.

Brace clamped his hands on his hips. "Hey, I just met Dory, my relief person for lunch break. She's adorable...but why didn't you tell me?"

She waded up her wax paper plate, trying to catch at least a fly or two in the process. "How would you like to be introduced by your least admirable trait?" She shot the wad at the closest trashcan and still missed, so she had to retrieve it for a direct dunk.

"Uh, How's this? Please meet my friend Brace. He can't keep his dirty socks off the floor." He lunged, trying to grab her waist.

She dodged him and laughed, making her way to the pick-up window to wait for his order.

"I shouldn't have tipped you off about that sock problem, as it puts me in negative light."

"Not after your tripping act this morning," she replied. "Go ahead, strew your socks." The serving window slid up and a paper boat appeared, filled with his hot dog and fries. She grabbed a sheet of wax paper to shield it from the insect world and held it out to him, nodding toward the condiment bar. "Kurtis has requested the honor of our presence at Lemur Island, so I thought you could picnic over there."

"Most excellent, let's go. I've never been close to the lemurs before. Do they have adequate show potential?" They left the shade of the lunch pavilion and walked by the albino alligator tent where Brace had to detour and take a glance.

She gave him a chance to catch up. "What should I say about lemurs and their show potential? They possess a clingy sort of confidence. You know, charisma with a tail."

"Nothing wrong with charisma," he said, taking a drink from his soda.

She started to say something but held back, having already argued this point with Leta. Maybe he'd see a little bit of a familiar tendency acted out on the rocks of Lemur Island. It could be cathartic, in a "know thyself" sort of way.

Kurtis waved as he released his last two customers back across the gated bridge. He soon pulled out the guitar case that waited in the wings. The musician strummed several chords, vocalizing in tune. The lemurs reacted to the new threat. While most of the adults froze in place, a sentinel climbed the tallest rock to keep watch.

Paisley settled cross-legged in a shady spot by the water's edge and a nearby fish came to the surface for a handout. She watched the small mammals with interest. Maybe they'd never heard music before.

Brace plopped down next to her trying to protect his food and drink from jostling. He bowed for his blessing and looked up in time to catch the start of the song.

A mid-tempo folk song resonated from the island and Kurtis carried it solidly through to the comical end, at which point the twin juveniles approached him and had to climb on.

She motioned for another number and he chose something with a faster beat. The twins began to wrestle and fell to the ground. Brace caught a stitch trying to stifle his laugh due to a mouth full of hot dog, but the rollick had entertainment value aplenty.

When the song ended, Paisley had an idea that might improve response across the age gap. "Can you try baiting some of the adults over, Kurt?"

He nodded and reached in his apron for the dried cranberries he sold to customers in exchange for two tokens. After his shoulders resembled a five-star general's, he launched into the state song. By the chorus of "Home, home on the range," he had grown lemur-heavy with four adults sitting on his lap.

She joined him for an impromptu duet for the last chorus. "Stimulus and response—I think you can train them through repetition. Soon they'll associate your singing with a treat."

"What about the rest of us?" Brace questioned. "Got any bait for us?" A mischievous look swept his face, evidence that he enjoyed a good-humored taunt.

"Try ear plugs," Kurtis suggested with a laugh.

"Hey, it might be fun to frolic with 'Madagascar' sound track tunes, since lemurs star in that kid flick. I like to move it, move it," Brace sang out, adding some rowing hand movements.

Kurtis shrugged. "Don't know if I ever watched that one, but I'm willing to give it a try."

"Future man party in order here," Brace replied. "Got a DVD player? I'll find a video and we'll jam on some ideas. Let me touch base with my meal-slurping junior comrades at Leta's, and I'll get back to you in a flash."

Recognizing his networking capabilities, she wondered what Brace could accomplish, given the proper resources and the sky as the limit. Her expression must have tipped him off, as he returned the look of admiration and downed his last French fry. "We'd better get back on the job, Kurtis. Let the critters warm up to the music. Brace may be right about keeping it up-tempo. We can save 'Home on the Range' as an encore piece for crowd participation or something."

"See you later, albino alligator," Brace added, shoving a fistful of knuckles his way. Kurtis bumped his fist back at them and they left the island nation for duty back on the mainland. "A duet partner for him would be a nice addition," he said under his breath as they merged onto the sidewalk by the rhino enclosure. "That way they could play tug-of-war for the lemurs' interest and make it even more comical for their audience."

"Yours is always the perspective of maximum showmanship."

"Not always," he replied with a subtle smile.

She somehow wanted to believe him, if only she could.

Chapter 8

Pretending to need a few more cosmos for her bouquet, Paisley lingered by the clothesline pole while Brace finished his reps. Every now and then, a wink would shoot her way and she collected them in her heart like a fistful of flowers. Time wound down before midweek service at church and the smell of simmering pickle relish wafted across the backyard.

Finding a lingering larkspur to add some blue to her bunch, she plucked it and straightened to find Leta hastening down the back walkway. When Brace released his grip and hit the ground in fluidity of motion, it seemed like they were coming at her from all sides. She met her landlady part way and Brace stalked her.

Leta wrung her hands in her apron, a reaction that didn't typically bode well. "Something terrible has happened to the Re-Occupy people out at the stockyards. The story's coming up next on the local news. I thought you two might want to catch it."

Brace's countenance changed and the leader trapped inside stepped up. "I knew Leland couldn't be trusted," he muttered, shouldering past her on the narrow walkway.

She placed her arm around Leta's waist and let the return hug keep her worries at bay. Brace lived here now and liked his job. Re-Occupy wasn't his concern any longer and certainly didn't pose any threat to her. So why did it feel like it all of a sudden?

They stepped through the sunroom to find Brace had maximized the volume, as he stood in front of the modest TV. An advertisement for the bank's annual fun run ended and the news anchor reappeared. Leta slipped behind the counter and kept her hot water canner from boiling over by lifting the lid. Paisley moved next to Brace, but opted for no contact while they waited for the news. When the anchor mentioned Dodge City, a knot tightened in her stomach. A remote reporter stood in front of the county hospital to render his report and the knot doubled.

"Members of the Re-Occupy Movement were hospitalized today after contamination of drinking water was blamed for widespread sickness among the group. Our exclusive interview with Seth Granger, owner of the Granger Stockyard being picketed, tells us more of what transpired."

Paisley was unable to blink. The world tilted a little out of control and she despised the feeling.

Brace sank to the arm of Leta's recliner, his eyes searching the screen. A gray-haired man stood before the camera hat in hand, his face washed with genuine concern for the situation.

"We'd been meeting and talking with the Re-Occupy folks all morning, allowing them to camp up the hill from the stockyard. Nobody here had an inkling about the contaminated water, but between the heat and open conditions, they were all stricken and had to be brought to Mercy Hospital. We're just as shaken up about this as the next fellow, and Granger Stockyards has offered to cover the medical expenses incurred. Let's just hope these young people can be up and on their way in no time."

Brace made a vicious throaty sound as the coverage switched back to the newsroom. A 4-H story followed and the audio tiptoed down to normal levels.

"Church starts in less than half an hour," Leta said. "We'll have the congregation pray and see how the Lord leads. Those kids need some help, that's for sure."

By his expression, Brace was already a hundred miles away, possibly coming up with his own plan. An abyss opened between them and she fell into it. Struggling, it occurred to her that she should offer something. Making the words come out proved to be another matter. "We could take up a love offering and deliver it in a rescue caravan."

A blank stare careened from his tense blue eyes. Sympathetic clucks came from the kitchen as a timer went off and Leta hoisted the canning rack from the hot water bath.

"God help me, I've got to do something," Brace mumbled, his voice trailing off like a raft losing air. "At least they have medical care right now when they need it."

"That Granger guy looks genuine," she added, trying to appease his apprehensions. "His promise to cover the hospital bill is a blessing. At least there won't be debt."

Brace backed away at her last comment, like she had struck him with a poison dart or something. "I'll… go get ready for church," he stammered, leaving the room.

His stunned look hung in the room like an inappropriate act, making her wonder what button she'd inadvertently pushed with what she'd said. Hadn't she tried to be empathetic? Off-balance, she glanced at Leta who now stood behind a wall of relish-filled pint jars all standing in a row.

The sound of a sealing lid pinged like a promise and Leta gave a tiny clap. "It'll all come together, dearie. Trust God more when the world seems out-of-control. It's what he's best at."

"I feel for Brace, Leta. They left him for dead in our parking lot, voted out of power and cut off from everything he cared about for the previous two months."

"And now he cares about something else. But he won't leave them for dead in return, I guarantee you that." Steam rose from the sink as the cook discarded the water bath, once full of purpose, but now just a pot of hot water making the fan work harder to keep the place cool.

The sink gurgled with the deluge and her stomach related as she turned to run upstairs for a precious few minutes to freshen up her appearance. One look at her drooping bouquet reminded her that the plucked flowers should have been in water right away. She knew what that meant symbolically. They would have to help Re-Occupy sooner than later.

~

Torn between needing to kneel before God and wanting to impulsively run to the rescue, Brace arrived at church a man divided. He sought out Pastor Steve right away and asked for special intercessory prayer for the Re-Occupy members. He'd barely been able to eat, but Leta insisted he keep up his strength, in case God called on him like Gideon. Unsure of the biblical reference, he did know that he was sitting on "go" and had to stay ready for the signal.

Kurtis strummed his guitar and led the group in a mellow series of worship songs. The slower rhythm matched his pensive mood, and he chose to worship because it was the right thing to do. He needed God more than God needed him. On the final song, he raised one arm toward heaven, like a rock climber questing for the summit. Pawnee Rock came to mind and the Holy Spirit's assurance came over him in comfort. He balled his fist and buried it into his sternum as the pastor led the prayer that began the message. When he sat down, Paisley came and sat with him, a peace over her countenance reassuring him.

"Let's talk about dependence on God," the pastor began. "It's not the message I prepared, but it's certainly the one most on my heart tonight. The provision of God meets our every need. Answer back in the affirmative if you can personally testify to his care."

A chorus of positive responses echoed back, including some spirited hallelujahs from the back. Brace's whispered "yes" got drowned out, but it was there with the rest.

"God works in ways we can't begin to understand. Somebody gets sick and it draws the fellow next to him closer to the heart of God. Another might get promoted and find his sphere of influence expanded, so he can give a testimony of God's faithfulness to more people. A baby is born and suddenly a crusty-hearted grandpa wants to make the world a better place for the child to grow up, starting with his own commitment to God. We're connected, aren't we? Your trouble becomes a trouble shared, your joy doubles when you pass it on to others. This has to be one of the mysteries of God, because even in autumn when the prairie grasses are sewn together by those teeny spider webs that float on the wind, mankind cannot see how interconnected we are."

Beyond the lump that formed in his throat, something settled down deep in Brace's heart. He knew nothing about those referenced spider webs, had never seen autumn sweep over a land of grass and flat horizons, but suddenly nothing in the world seemed more appealing to him. If he had to throw a name at what he was experiencing, he'd have to call it longing for a home.

His breath became labored and he leaned forward, cradling his head into his arms on the table. Within seconds, a hand came to his back and he knew it belonged to Paisley. The longing grew and she became swirled into it, like one couldn't happen without the other. Helpless to steer the sensation, he let it float around his chest and lay claim to who he was becoming.

"We've received news that our friends from the Re-Occupy Movement have been stricken with contaminated water at their stop by the stockyards in Dodge City," Steve said. A murmur followed as members of the congregation became aware of the situation.

Brace sat up to witness their reaction firsthand.

Steve stood, placed his Bible on the stool, and began to wander back and forth in front of the congregation.

"We called them our friends just a week or so ago, didn't we? Took them food, invited them to church. Let them camp in our beloved wildlife park."

The thumb resting on his back twitched at the mention of the park and he knew the inclusion had landed on Paisley with a direct hit.

"But did we show them Jesus?" he asked, raising his voice. He pointed back to the stool where the Bible rested and the implication became raw and real. "Some might say it's not our problem now. They're in Dodge City, aren't they? Surely some godly saints there will be charitable and get those lofty-minded kids back up and on their way, won't they?"

The room fell silent as his eyes misted, helpless and mute to alter the course of history.

"Or could this somehow be our second chance? Somehow? Some way?" Steve asked, his voice trailing into a whisper. "The Maker of water from rocks, he who draws water from seeps and springs in the hills so the flocks will have provision, gave these traveling gypsies tainted water to halt them in their tracks. We might ask ourselves *why*? Are these the tensile webs of interconnectedness? Maybe...Somebody gets sick and it draws the next fellow closer to the heart of God, right?" The pastor strolled to the far side of the fellowship hall and someone audibly sobbed.

A fire started burning in Brace's chest and he fought the urge to run out.

"Ananias and Sapphira didn't get a second chance, did they? They held back and got called on the carpet for it, so it almost seems like cheating for us to be offered a second opportunity to show Christ to Re-Occupy. That's God's grace, my friends, his character of generosity extending to us another chance to do something for this band who happened to travel through Podunk little Pawnee Rock. Lucky for us he left behind a tie to bind us with the group, a web of interconnectedness that links us with this second chance. Brace Cordan, come up here, brother."

The sound of his name seared his ears and something quaked inside. Whatever this call-to-action was, his body had to obey, so he stood and stepped to the front in grainy motion. His sinuses ached from holding back the tears, and by the time he made it up front, his teeth grated so hard his jaw hurt. He didn't feel like a spider web, but if God wanted him to be a connection, he wouldn't fight it. Obedience—though lacking understanding—equated to faith. He had that much, but little else.

Steve's right arm found his shoulder and tugged him to his side. "Brace has confided to me that he feels called by God to go help Re-Occupy. What would that look like if we sent him as our ambassador? Should we offer the basics of God's provision: food, water, shelter, and space? Should we send Bibles or dollar bills? Should we go with him or should he bring them back? Speak out if God has impressed something on your hearts."

"Food and water," one man answered. Steve nodded and held out one hand, begging for the next input. A woman cried into a tissue and the man beside her stood.

"For God's sake and for our own, bring them back, those that will come. Our Travis is there with them, and he's breaking his mother's heart staying gone like this."

Guilt flitted into Brace's mind knowing he had taken that son's job at the park, but his heart somehow deflected the burden because it didn't seem to be relevant.

The man sat down and another stood. "We need to take up a collection—a love offering. That would sponsor bus tickets home to those who want them, and meet needs we can't even begin to know or understand. Only God knows, but we can be his agents through our offerings."

Steve nodded, waiting for anyone else to stand up. Several murmurs stirred the crowd but no one else spoke. "Brace doesn't even own a vehicle," Steve said in earnest candor. "Is there another heart being called out there? Whom shall we send and who will go for us?"

Brace recognized the scriptural call and knew the answer somehow would validate whether God was orchestrating this or if it smacked of manmade contrivance. Paisley had her scout program in town tomorrow, so she was out. This couldn't be some personal favor anyway. It had to fall as the authentic call of God. The silence made it difficult to draw a breath until a large bulk shattered the pause.

"Here am I, send me, Lord," Kurtis sang. He strummed his guitar while nodding to the other church members who echoed him in repeating the phrase. The worship song continued in a round while two men got up with empty flower pots and began collecting the love offering. Kurtis wandered up front beside him while Steve took the opportunity to reach for his wallet.

Something akin to wings unfurled inside Brace's chest as he soaked in the faith moment that made him want to fly. He was an aerialist after all, at least in fleshly effort. He had a feeling he stood on the verge of finding out what his man-of-faith act would be, as ambassador back to his Re-Occupy people. Glancing over in Paisley's direction, he saw that she'd been crying. Too bad tears had a see-through element to them, as it didn't speak clearly of happiness or sadness. Knowing his swirly-girl, it could be both.

~

Ruts cut across her psyche again as she traveled Highway 56, the historic Santa Fe Trail. Paisley wouldn't be the first woman who had to jettison something out of her wagon to make the trip onward. The Girl Scout Hut appeared to her left and she shifted her turn signal on reluctantly. She'd brought a cold-blooded reptile with her today, a juvenile Gila monster, because she wasn't in the mood for a warm fuzzy. This was her job and she'd do it with committed determination, regardless of how long after-hours it lasted.

That Brace rode with Kurtis ever westward to reacquaint himself with his old troupe at this very moment shouldn't give her any reason to brood. On a mission from God that she supported, such work should not be questioned. That it took him from her proximity and back toward them stirred unsettling doubts nonetheless, making it a matter of the heart. Paint hers black, lonesome black.

Chapter 9

Brace shoved through the main doors of the regional hospital. "You record and I'll bestow." Kurtis joined him at the information counter where two senior volunteers eyed them with candid suspicion. *This is what happens when the media gets involved.* He gave the closest woman a genuine smile. "I hope the two of you can help us today, so that we can multiply that kindness to our friends in the Re-Occupy group."

She folded her hands to conceal her desk blotter. "How may I assist you?"

"We've been sent by the Congregational Church of Pawnee Rock," he replied.

"I'm Kurtis Morehead, Music Minister," his assistant interjected in a steady voice.

"And I'm Brace Cordan, ambassador for this community aid outreach effort—and former president of the Re-Occupy Movement. When they moved to Dodge City twelve days ago, I stayed behind in Pawnee Rock, by the grace of God."

"And now you want to reconnect, is that right, Mr.

Cordan?"

"Yes. To help them in their time of need…"

"We've brought a love offering with us to fund bus tickets back home for the weary of suffering," Kurtis added, aiding his cause.

"And the folks of Pawnee Rock are waiting to take the others in, anyone willing to return and get back on their feet. We have one vehicle and can rent another if we need to, depending on how many accept our offer."

"We have been restricting access to that wing, but I can ask the director for an exception, since you know the patients and have come to lend aid."

Brace took a moment to read her nametag. "Bless you, Miss Rose. Would you please call and try to get us that access? No one deserves to suffer by themselves so far away from home." This time when she looked up at him, he detected a trace of Christian charity in her face as she fingered the push-button phone on the desktop. Something told him to keep his gaze locked on her, although Kurtis kicked at his right foot below the counter.

"Excuse the interruption, Mr. Anderson. It's Rose up front. I have a couple of relief workers representing a church back in Pawnee Rock where the Re-Occupy patients were previously. Their former leader is here with relief money and wants permission to access the group members."

A pause opened and he knew the decision weighed in the balance.

"Yes, sir. He looks like the real thing," Rose replied, glancing back up at him.

Hope swelled in his chest and he leaned over the counter, fighting the urge to collect the woman in a big hug.

"All right, sir. I'll let them know."

"Connie, get these two men badges for G wing, pronto," she said. "Mr. Cordan, you'll have to wash your hands outside the wing before entering. Follow this main hall until it forks after the second set of doors. Go left at the fork and look for the orange G Wing signs. I'm calling the nurses' station down there now, advising them to admit you both. There are two hours left in visitor's hours this evening, so work quickly and may God guide your efforts."

"Bless you, Miss Rose. I could just kiss you for this." Brace took his nametag from her helper. Her cheeks blushed and she made a notation on the blotter as he put on the lanyard.

When she looked up again, her eyes were misted. "No, bless you both young men, for caring enough to come. Off you go, and not another minute wasted." Her demeanor softened with a smile as they shoved away from the counter.

The first set of doors parted automatically and Kurtis broke the silence. "Great job, Brace. Now help me out in here as we make our rounds. Tell me who's who so I can keep the ledger with discretion. Remember, we can take three people back with us. Travis can fit three more—if I can talk him into coming home. Any more takers and we'll have to rent something for you to drive back."

"What's with the shoe kick, man? Enough people are hurt already. We're the rescuers, so tread lightly." "Sorry, dude. I've got big feet. That's my secret signal that I'm praying for you, when I tap your right foot."

The second set of doors stood before them and he

halted as they opened. "What does it mean if you kick my left foot?" he teased, getting into this tag-team thing.

"Uh, let's say it means….move the heck on over," Kurtis replied, giving him a sheepish grin. "You're not the only one with boyish charm, you know."

"Oh, I see how it is." He zeroed in on the nurses' station. His fingers found the business end of the lanyard and his smile lingered long enough to make a deposit on the duty nurse. "We're asking to visit the Re-Occupy group. I'm Brace and this is Kurtis."

"Thank you both for coming. There's been a widespread misery over this bunch that's been tearing our hearts out all night. The tide has turned, but they're all weak as kittens. We've just started solid food this evening, and when I say solid, that's stretching it."

"I'm acutely familiar with the applesauce road to recovery," Brace replied. "That's how I got left behind in the first place, but now God is using my stomach purge for good. Tell us how to start, as we need to contact every member to find out who'll accept some help."

"Plans are in place for the East Coast members, as Mr. Gardner from the stockyards has chartered a bus for that portion of the group. They leave tomorrow morning at shift change."

"He was the fellow on the news, wasn't he?" Brace asked, hoping she might elaborate.

"That's right." She tucked a diagram of the hall onto a clipboard. She handed it to him and he passed to Kurtis, thinking it would help hide his paperwork. "He's a generous benefactor here and serves on the hospital's board of trustees like his father did. Mr.

Gardner is absolutely sick over what's happened to these young people. He just left at dinnertime so we could get them served. And he'll be here in the morning when the bus loads. Sorry you missed him, as he would have wanted to connect."

"Let me leave him a note then." Reaching into his pocket, he produced a paper folded in quarter and scrawled a couple of lines of sentiment on the back. After all, the draft announcement for the park's Shakespeare Festival could be reproduced, but his chance to thank the stockyard owner could not. He signed and put Kurtis' cell number with it, hoping he'd call.

"First up looks like Chloe Rinehart," Kurtis said, reading the hall chart.

"Chloe has been the worst," the nurse confided with a deft look. "Her Crone's condition exacerbated the contamination symptoms. She's weak but could be released, given enough care."

Brace exhaled in agony, realizing too late that her thin profile had hinted at something internally amiss, if he'd only known how to read it. Kurtis searched him out with a probing look.

"Folks are waiting back home to give every degree of care needed," Brace assured her. "Let's get this rescue party started."

His lighthearted reply broke her sullenness, and she shoved the door open with a twinkle in her eyes.

The antiseptic smell that met them on the other side brought him down a notch. Suffering never respected a smiling face, and he internalized the scent warning with caution. Still he had peace beyond his own ability, and he walked in armed with that, along with the resolute need to intervene for the good.

Entering the first room, Brace found a young man folded into a caregiver's chair looking like death warmed over. Stunned not to see Chloe there, he froze midstride.

Kurtis shouldered around him and a light flickered on the man's face. He stood and Kurtis wrapped him in a buddy lock that would have toppled a grizzly bear. "Travis, your folks are worried out of their minds." He popped his big brute hands on the frail man's shoulders as though to gauge his endurance. "The church sent us to bring you guys back, as many as will come. This is our lead ambassador, Brace Cordan. Brace, meet Travis Burke, hometown boy gone AWOL."

"Your reputation as a harmonica player extraordinaire precedes you, Travis," he replied, holding back the fact that he'd assumed his job at the park.

"Time for the Shakespeare Festival, isn't it?" he replied with ease. "Thought I was going to dodge that bullet this year, but now it seems mild compared to what we've been through. Chloe's been awful. It tears my heart out to see her suffer like that."

"Brace?" A female voice floated through the white curtain that hung along the left side of the room.

Travis nodded him over and he swept the divider back to see the withered version of an old friend.

"You coming to rejoin Re-Occupy?"

"Hey there, Chloe," Brace replied, the cinder of reconnection starting a fire in his gut. "No. I'm here to bring you guys back. The townsfolk want to take you in at Pawnee Rock to nurse you back to health. We're heading back tonight. I want you to think about coming home with Travis. His folks are part of the congregation sponsoring this outreach. We've got money, food, and a place for you to stay. We'll even try to help find you jobs. These are good people, Chloe—salt of the earth people. They've taken me in. I have a job at the wildlife park now…"

"So great for you, Brace. Your student loan…" she offered, short of breath.

He took her fragile hand in his to help convince her. "I know, Chloe. There's more for all of you, trust me. The summer circuit ends here. It's crash and burn for Re-Occupy, but not for you. Come, let us take care of you. Meet Travis's family and the other good folks back in Pawnee Rock. I've got money to give Travis for gas, so you two talk about it and let me know before I leave. Okay?" He watched a tear roll down from the outer corner of her eye as she lay there so helplessly weak.

"Bring me Travis," she replied, releasing his hand.

He stepped back out, swallowing down the emotion as Kurtis pushed the Pawnee Rock native into the private zone.

"Things never change, do they?" another female asked. The curtain on the right wiggled as the occupant gave a hollow laugh. "Chloe gets all the male attention. Is anybody coming to rescue poor little ol' me?"

The question didn't hang in the air for long, as the velvet voice seemed to break something loose inside his assistant who shouldered into position.

"Is that Mimi Sims, begging to be rescued?" Brace teased, pulling back the divider. The familiar half-blond, half-brunette jester came into view and slid down his recovery zone like eye salve. "Look at you,

Mimi, taking a time out when there's so much to do."

Kurtis inched closer. He seemed awe stricken.

"Easy for you to say, Brace, as you took your sick leave early instead of taking on the beef industry," she replied with coy baiting. "Sad to admit, but this is the best bed I've had all summer."

Kurtis cleared his throat to get his attention, tapping on the clipboard.

Brace thought the guy was double-checking his recordkeeping sheet for accuracy until he got the first tap on the foot. The *left* foot. "Hey, Mimi. This is my friend from the wildlife park and church, Kurtis Morehead. Kurt, meet Mimi Sims."

The big guy hunkered over the patient as something mutual seemed to exchange between the two.

"Zowey, honey," Mimi crooned. "You can rescue me anytime."

"Ma'am, my distinct pleasure," Kurtis replied, his voice hitting a couple of unsure notes. The pencil rolled from the clipboard and landed on her bed. The record keeper became all thumbs attempting its retrieval. Fortunately, the patient had focus and twirled the writing utensil in her fingers until he took it from her, mesmerized.

He'd have to spring the rescue message himself again. "Mimi, come back with us. The people of Pawnee Rock want anyone that feels so led to come back. We stand ready to meet your needs during your recovery. Why, you could even help us with the festival coming up. You've always got a song on your lips anyway. We can give you an admiring audience, plus get Kurtis here a duet partner for his act on Lemur Island."

His assistant looked between the two of them like collusion had formed outside of his input, but a smile soon crept across his face at the possibilities.

Mimi meowed like a leopard kitten and pointed insistently at the clipboard. "Put me down as an escapee." She combed her fingers through her bangs. "So, you got a seat in that rescue vehicle for me?"

Kurtis stepped in front of Brace to get closer. "Right by my side." He placed his big hand on her head right over her part. His prayer asked for her release from the hospital and for her return to strength with passionate commitment.

Outdone, Brace felt like a charlatan for a short minute. They were here to make a difference, and they had significant progress. He turned to exit and a hand clamped on his shoulder.

"We'll both head back with you tonight," Travis said, his eyes crinkling in the corners.

"Great," he exclaimed, meaning it from the bottom of his heart. "Get some rest, then. We'll stop by when it's time to pull out. I've got gas money, so we'll stop on the way out of town. I hope you can feel the hand of God in all of this."

"I do. No, we both do," he admitted, seeming weary from the road of independence. "Will the nurse release Chloe? I mean, she's been pretty bad off."

"I already have the nurse's word that Chloe can go, if she chooses to. She's making a special case."

Kurtis joined them, dialing a number on his cell phone. Once the connection came through, he handed the phone to his boyhood friend. "Let your folks know, so they'll be ready for Chloe's needs." Kurtis nodded at the phone.

Travis swallowed his pride and took the phone, lowering into the chair for a slice of humble pie. Emotions in the room thickened as he spoke the first reconnecting words.

As Kurtis gravitated back over to Mimi's side of the room, Brace wandered out the door. How many more connections would be made or missed tonight? A heavy mantle weighed on his shoulders and the apostles from the Book of Acts came to mind. Anointing came with a heaping helping of responsibility when the decisive tide pulled toward an eternity with or without God.

Kurtis appeared, sliding his phone back into his shirt pocket. "I'm amped," he said, showing him two circles for one stop on the hall diagram.

"Hold back on the charm and charisma a little, Mr. Amped," he cautioned. "Not everybody will be as subject to your charm as Mimi."

"She's amazing," he replied without a hint of shame. "Next room is Les and Lars Caruthers. They sound like brothers."

"Basketball playing twins," he said. "And I've got just the right hook for them."

"Does he stand about six foot-seven and preach on Sundays?" Kurtis guessed.

"Don't you know it," he replied, entering the next room with a tiny knock. "Anybody here want to meet a San Antonio Spurs superstar?" Two men yelped for consideration at the same time and from the corner of his eye, he saw Kurtis raise the pencil in place.

~

The baby Gila monster resided in his cage again, and the Scout hut had cleared of its junior occupants. Paisley slowed her preparation for departure as her thoughts flitted to Brace, wondering how much success he was experiencing. Papier-mâché animal forms dotted the tables, left to dry between sessions by their creators. Walking back toward the storage closets, she smiled as several Gila monsters took form in the line-up.

"Rae Anne?" she called, hoping to say her goodbyes. A feeling of unfinished business came over her and Brace came to mind again. Getting free proved more difficult as time passed.

"In here, Paisley," the troop leader called, followed by a loud clatter as aluminum struck the floor. She followed the groans and entered the closet to find a row of cots had shifted onto the woman's thighs, leaving her off-balance with two sets of paints in hand threatening to collide. "Help?" she chirped, peeping out from one side.

Scurrying into rescue mode, she couldn't figure out why the cots seemed to be calling out to her beyond the immediate emergency, but they did anyway. A vision of Kurtis' truck filled to the brim with Re-Occupy members came to her mind-eye and the cots transformed into welcomed commodities. She shoved them back into alignment and formulated her approach for the loan. "Want some walking room in here?" she asked, testing the waters.

"That would be a dream-come-true. Do you need some cots?"

"Our church has sent a team out west to rescue the Re-Occupy members that fell sick at the Dodge City stockyards. Some may choose to accept our offer to come back to Pawnee Rock for their recovery. I don't know how many, or if they'll even come at all."

"More will come than you think. Take as many as

you can fit in your car."

Paisley recognized good advice when she heard it. She could fold down the back seats and extend the hatch's capacity. That put the junior Gila monster in front with her, but that way they could keep an eye on each other. Not like Brace, who was out-of-sight but not out-of-mind, and certainly not out-of-heart. A solitary pang of abandonment became all she had time for, as the cots began to follow her out of the closet, one by one.

Chapter 10

Folks Paisley had known all her life comprised the semi-circle of people around him. Yet tonight it seemed that she'd know them to a greater depth, as they stood at a spiritual juncture ready to reach out with the connectedness Pastor Steve had challenged them with. Doubt blew through her like the summer breeze that tugged at the cottonwoods, rattling their leaves in the night. Anybody could do familiar, but who embraced the stranger when ushered into the unknown?

"All I'm asking is that you live and love like the New Testament church," Steve said, his voice slipping into the dark as midnight approached.

A stab of headlights pierced the parking lot as first one vehicle then another rounded the turn off the highway and advanced toward the church. Paisley held her breath but remembered to pray a beggar's plea that the in-rush wouldn't exceed the outpouring of human compassion, lest God have to magnify their effort on the spot. She opened her eyes and realized that God had already brought the increase, as they had never cared this much about anything collectively prior to this night.

The lead vehicle blinked its high beams on for a split second. It seemed like an angel had slid down from heaven, her heart became so open and welcoming. Several men trotted forward as though to meet the truck and physically bring it into orbit around the church building. The hushed voice of expectancy lifted the wait to a higher level, and the anticipation tasted like a fruit of the Spirit, along with joy, peace, and patience. Leta began clapping and hopping up and down like a little girl standing at the feet of Jesus. Paisley clapped without giving it a second thought and soon the entire group applauded.

Steve held his arms out like a crucifix and the truck pulled up to his commanding presence, shifting the crowd.

Suddenly on the second row, Paisley struggled to see as the vehicle door opened. A cab light revealed a truck full of people. Someone in the group gasped and another let out a hallelujah.

"We have Re-Occupy with us," Brace reported, "nine strong, plus your two ambassadors of goodwill."

Steve strode toward him and pulled him up into an embrace like a long-lost hero, making a lump form in Paisley's throat.

"The East coast members already had a bus chartered and will leave for home in the morning. The rest accepted money for gas or bus tickets to their destinations, but we had enough to help every last one."

"Praise God on high," Steve called, celebrating the outreach victory.

Kurtis appeared next from the driver's seat, holding a delicate woman only half awake. "Everybody, please meet Mimi Sims." He swung around so everyone could see and the girl rallied with a slight smile.

Paisley stifled a sob when her mother stepped forward.

"We'd like to be the first to offer as host," she stated, and her father stepped forward to make it mutually official. Steve pointed to the church secretary who recorded the information as fast as she could write. Paisley knew the adoptee would likely get her vacated bedroom, but not an ounce of possessiveness tainted the union.

Brace retrieved a pack from the truck bed and handed it to her father. When Kurtis disappeared into the dark depths of the parking lot with them, Brace pulled the next visitors out from the cab's jump seats. Paisley had a bad case of double vision.

"Meet Les and Lars Caruthers, basketball players extraordinaire," Brace said. A few welcomes echoed back from the group, but two installments must have proven too much for the majority because no sponsor stepped up. Finally, a spunky figure wiggled free from the back line and Paisley recognized the pastor's wife.

"We've come to appreciate that particular game at our house," she teased. "Steve and I would be grateful to have you both at our place."

The twins turned toward the pastor who had already broken emotionally at his wife's independent gesture, swiping away the tears with the back of his massive hands. "Yes, it would be our honor," he conceded. The men bucked their knuckles together in triumph, which brought a hearty chuckle from the group all around.

Brace led them to the truck's bed and fished out their belongings, handing a bedroll to the pastor.

Tucking it under the crook of his arm, the pastor gathered the men, one to a side around him. "Who's next?"

"Travis Donlinger, the errant, returning home if you'll have me," a voice called.

Paisley clapped her hands over her mouth as a cry of relief escaped, joined by other gasps and exclamations as her former workmate appeared pushing a wheelchair. "And this is Chloe Rinehart, my girlfriend. She's been the sickest of all and needs the most TLC."

"We'd like to ask you to come back home, son," Mr. Donlinger confessed, following his wife in stepping from the group. "And Effie here will take Chloe. She's a nurse and the best one fitted to provide special care. Plus, that would place Chloe right next door, so you can visit her all you like. And another thing, Travis. We got you a job working with your brother-in-law at his auto repair shop in Great Bend. It's a flexible schedule, whatever you're up to until you get your strength back. We want you, son. The whole town wants you back, so there isn't any shame in coming home, only love—and lots of it."

Paisley watched the reuniting scene in tears, as nothing that beautiful had transpired in front of her in a long time. Even Chloe stood and tried to get locked into the group embrace, but it soon became obvious the young woman had been through a great trial.

Travis faltered having filled the part of the strong boyfriend for too long, but when his knees buckled, his father's steady arm was there to lift him back up. Their group moved off toward the family car, and the rest of the passengers came forward to be introduced.

One by one, each member was adopted by a resident

and swept away to a sound night's sleep, with Leta snagging two Cornhuskers, Weston and Riley, for the crow's nest. Brace helped load their things in her antique car as Paisley bid farewell to Pastor Steve and his new teammates.

She overheard the promise to be right home as Leta passed Brace, leaving the two of them alone in the parking lot.

"Here I am, as penniless as I was the last time I came to town," he joked, sending her a knowing look.

She stepped toward him and gave the heavenly hosts a glance as Leta's headlights dimmed with distance.

"And yet you have so much more," she replied, conferring the words like a blessing. "Want a ride home, Mr. Ambassador?"

"Maybe a slow ride home," he replied, looking at her through heavy eyelids. Fatigue and victory seemed to be fighting it out for his conscious state.

"Looks like I get to rescue the rescuer," she teased, bumping his side with her arm.

"Praise God and pass the pillow," he replied, lowering his head onto her shoulder.

Somewhere in the blackness of night, her hand found his and he held it to his chest like a long-cherished possession, making the agony of abandonment melt from her memory. Nothing else felt like this, and nothing else could. She opened the passenger door for him and touched the downy waves that graced the top of his head as he lowered into the seat with a moan.

"Home," he repeated in a trance-like stupor.

She crossed to the driver's seat, visualizing the balcony and backyard that stood between her home and his, a distance that seemed too far apart for her heart.

~

The lorikeets played like toddlers in a sandbox this morning, which would serve the Friday crowd well. Brace glowed with validation when Marty announced a ladies' group from Stafford had responded to his initial marketing campaign and would be touring later this afternoon. If the birds would cooperate, he could give them a preview of the festival act, hovering bird platform and all.

With his father due to arrive hauling his gymnastics equipment this weekend, he'd soon have his rings set up in the aviary and could practice on his iron man pose. Working that position to horizontal would be an open invitation to perch and a real crowd pleaser, if his shoulder muscles could pull it off. Looking up, he caught Paisley striding past the cage, shoving the food cart toward Lemur Island and the petting zoo.

"What's the big hurry?"

She turned to him with tears brimming in her eyes, stopping the cart long enough to answer. "Marty sold the clouded leopard kittens yesterday while we were away." She tried to suck up the emotion. "It's not like he hasn't done it before, but it just seems so behind-the-back this time. I don't know what's wrong with me."

The cart started up again but not before he could shoulder out of the plastic curtain and step out to come alongside her. "You're tenderhearted because you care about the animals," he replied, hesitant to touch her while on the job but wanting to anyway. His hand gripped the cart instead. "You keep them alive on a daily basis, so it's natural you would resent anyone interfering with that. That's who you are, Paisley—the nurturer. Maybe you could channel that into your act."

"Maybe, like a woodland fairy in 'A Midsummer Night's Dream.'"

"That's the spirit. I'm thinking of doing a comedic spin on Othello. I'd like to call it O-Jell-o, if Leta could loan out my juvenile cohorts under her care. I need some henchmen with a certain unrefined skill set."

"Oh, yeah, the slurp brigade," she replied, dabbing the corner of her eye. "Guess you could offer the boys a pass to the event if you really need the help."

"I need my Desdemona, too. Could you do it for me? Throw a few dance swirls around my angry, jealous gymnastics?"

She leaned over the cart considering her options. "How are you planning to smother me, O-Jell-o? How about marshmallows? I'd like to die by marshmallows, if you please."

"Anything to keep my leading lady happy, so marshmallows it is," he conceded with a wink. He furrowed his brow considerably and looked up into her soft brown eyes. "How do I keep my henchmen from un-smothering you? That could be a problem, keeping them out of the marshmallow pile…"

"Impose a gelatin-only rule, sire. That should do. And we could use the larger pillow marshmallows, to make sure the birds don't try to ingest them."

He nodded as his thoughts ricocheted through the plotline. "Crackers will be Iago, and we'll use a narrator to tie the storyline together. It's perfect, except for the breach-of-trust stabbing from the original score. That would happen between us, of course."

"No way," she agreed with considerable disdain.

"Good, then I'll take my pitcher of nectar pleasure and get ready to thrill today's guests with my bird-training expertise.”

“Or simply let them enjoy the lorikeets cup-by-cup. That’s been our stand-by for ages.”

“I’ll resort to that between practices for my horizontal hold,” he teased, stepping back toward the aviary. “Hey, once the Re-Occupy folks get back on their feet, I’d like to incorporate them into the festival.”

“Great idea, Brace. I heard Kurtis has already asked Mimi to join him for a duet on Lemur Island. Mom’s giving her a part-time job with housecleaning at the hotel. She would still have her afternoons for crooning—so maybe Kurtis could do his job without distraction until she gets here.”

“Yeah, the big guy was slain at first sight, with her Siren voice luring his musical ear. I have a feeling about those two.”

“Hold that thought, Cupid. Your time’s better spent figuring out how to turn Shakespeare’s tale of jealous rage into a comedy filled with gelatin-romping.”

“Hey—maybe Amyl could put together a food cart with jigglers that day.” He pointed at her as he backed into the outer aviary door, balancing the pitcher in one hand.

“You’re just chock-full of good ideas, aren’t you O-Jell-o?”

“Watch your back, Desdemona. I might be gunning for your assistant director position,” he threatened with mock aggression. She threw her nose into the air and pranced away with a high step, giving him the last laugh.

He poured a row of cups a third full of nectar, and gave some thought to his practice routine about the time Crackers came walking through the no-trespass zone of the plastic curtain into the front foyer. Spilling some nectar onto the back of his hand, he stepped toward the bird and offered his limb as a perch.

"I'm the marshmallow," he conceded to his feathered betrayer. The bird licked his thumb like an attending remora as he pushed the curtain back to reintroduce the escapee to its habitat.

~

Paisley handed the fruit hash to Kurtis as he stood on the bridge to Lemur Island. The animal handler looked like something had run him over since he'd had a late night. She pulled the chicken parts out under the full radiation of the sun, so the last traces of freezer frost would disappear before her next stop—the albino alligator's tent.

"Is last night a do-over for you?" she asked, turning the cart around.

"Not at all, I made lots of new friends." He tugged his baseball cap lower on his brow.

"And a singing partner, right?" she teased. They'd known each other a long time, since elementary school. She thought they could talk about personal stuff.

"Hey, don't make me look bad in front of Mimi," he replied, gesturing with the feed container. "I have to up my game a bit, especially in the vocals department."

"You sound great. Just be yourself, for crying out loud, Kurtis. She'll like what she hears and sees, I guarantee it. If it's meant to be, I mean."

"God's doing something crazy here, right? First you meet Brace and now I have a chance with Mimi. What's up with all that?"

Her heart skipped a beat when Brace got brought into the equation. Re-Occupy had introduced a few elements outside of the regular formula, but as long as God's hand did the mixing, she wouldn't balk at the pairing up. No, balking didn't seem to be part of her emotional repertoire right now.

"God's hand and God's timing—both are on our side," she admitted. "Heaven help us not play the fool. Right now, I'm slated to play Desdemona to Brace's Othello in a comedic version where I suffocate under marshmallows in a regime of junior-sized gelatin-slurpers."

"And that's not playing the fool?" he asked with a laugh.

"So you're singing with lemurs cavorting on your head, but have the nerve to ask me that?" she sniped in full comeback mode. "We're in too deep already! God save the home folk." The bridge quaked under her feet as she left the lemur compound, unsteady and unready for what might lay ahead.

# Chapter 11

Brace had to re-boot his preconceived notions about the leisure of Saturdays, as the wildlife park was open for business and he had a job to do. Paisley left for the food prep room minutes ago. Today, his goal to get the flyer electronically airborne by the middle of July came due. If he hurried, he could achieve that feat and still have time to make the rounds with her.

Leaning over Marty's desk to get his computer up, Brace noticed a random scatter of chicken-scratched post-it notes in an ark around the monitor. He depressed the on switch and the computer came to life, adding a blue tint of lighting to the desk mess. The clouded leopard debacle came to mind and he thought about searching for the price tag per kitten in the notes, but it struck him as snooping, so he focused on the screen instead.

Marty had thrown a slight conniption last weekend when he'd asked for the password, but he'd held his ground, insisting that the marketing emphasis deserved access whether the director was in attendance or not. He couldn't operate from the auxiliary laptop without getting the Wi-Fi up, so he had to promise not to work from the main PC.

Pulling up the online service, he watched for the telltale posting of inbox e-mails and then switched the Wi-Fi over. A subject line from the bank in Great Bend caught his eye, indicating a transfer request out of the account had been completed. Maybe he'd mention that to Paisley, as it might be standard operating procedure for the park since it was part of a family-owned chain, even though it struck him as odd.

Brace shifted to the side table and centered on the laptop he used for marketing support. The screensaver came up after he plugged in the password, and he stared at the field of wildflowers that always made him think of Paisley. He'd better corral his thoughts this morning, or he could kiss making rounds with her good-bye. The idea of a kiss lingered in his bloodstream, seeping through him like a tonic. She had a way of making him feel alive like no one else, yet she seemed to be unaware of her effect on him. He smiled and clicked open the festival flyer file, thinking how his father might just bail him out of his predicament.

Fighting out of a personal prison of financial debt had no shout-out-loud to it, but he was coming at it with both fists held high. His paltry payout for one week's work would soon be joined by a full paycheck. Plus, his escalator clause kicked in yesterday when the ladies group put them more than ten percent over average attendance for the day. He made a note of the gate count provided daily by Cerise in a separate file, in case Marty objected and failed to pay. Three weeks' work would make a nice first payment on the student loan debt coming due next month. He'd pay early for release of his own incarcerated conscience, not to prove anything more. His dad was set to bring the paperwork tomorrow after church, along with the rings and his gear.

Collecting contacts to add to his distribution list took half an hour, and when the time popped up on the footer bar, he thought of Paisley and began to hurry. Remembering the contact information from the hospital in Dodge City, he added it to the list and felt satisfied. Scanning the flyer once more, he decided to add a notation about having support from the Re-Occupy immigrants. Paisley had called an evening get-together at Pawnee Rock Sunday night to take volunteer support and assign tasks for the festival. When thoughts of her rooftop dance drifted to mind, he had to hold his finger on the send command to stay on task. Exhaling a prayer, he sent the announcement electronically, and held his palms up off the keyboard like an innocent man.

Making his marketing deadline had been one thing, but making Paisley's austere food distribution schedule was quite another. He brought the laptop down and crossed over to Marty's computer to do the same. His focus fell on the bank communication, so he memorized the bank's name and exited. In the blink of an eye, the system closed and the computer went blank. The door banged behind him as he raced to find the fun part of his day.

~

Red eyes flashed as the chicken leg flicked through the air, and soon a set of vise-like teeth clamped down on the fleshy offering. Paisley wiped her hands and noted the condition of the water in the alligator's exhibit. They'd have to clean it first of the week. Maybe she could teach one of the Re-Occupy guys how to drain it. Footsteps padded up behind her, so she turned to find out who it was. Kurtis tipped his cowboy hat, reminding her that dress code had slipped a little on Saturdays in Marty's absence.

"Good morning, Lemur king," she said, noting his positive mood.

"Couldn't be a better morning," he replied, stepping up to secure his fruit apportionment for the lemurs. "I walked through on the kangaroo compound already. Needs a poop scoop."

"Yeah, we're getting behind with some of the cleanup. I noticed that the larger-than-usual crowd yesterday left Amyl with a pretty big trash mess under the pavilion. Brace is having some luck with his marketing outreach, which equates to added pressure on our resources."

"Maybe some of the Re-Occupy dudes can get hired as groundskeepers. The cost would be offset by the increased gate, so I don't think Marty would squawk about it."

"Marty squawks about every cost. I'm practically out of animal food after this weekend. Let me work on him Tuesday when he's fresh from his weekend off and clear-minded enough to entertain a new idea. I'm thinking about suggesting support three times a week."

"Sounds good. Now, let's figure out how to compensate the help we're getting from Re-Occupy for the festival. Do we pay for performers? Technicians? Crowd control? Venders?"

"Let's chat that up at the bonfire Sunday night and

see what they'd prefer. We have a budget, but it's fairly small, all things considered. I think it's a holdover from a decade ago."

"Got to go feed up my varmints. If they don't get to chow down early, I pity the first customer who traipses across that bridge."

"Especially the juveniles. They're crazy lately."

"Seems I like crazy," he replied, a sly smile sliding beneath the hat brim's shade.

A two-toned female singer crossed Paisley's mind and she knew what wave length he occupied. "Have a good day on your island kingdom," she teased as he waved her off. A puff blew into her ear as another meddler came to interrupt her routine. This one might be a tad more welcome, because she enjoyed the way his eyes sparkled like lake water.

Brace stood pouting like a three-year old. "You left without me."

She pressed his bottom lip in with the tip of her pinky, shoving the cart forward with her other hand. "Our gate is opening soon and the savages will run among us, so I have to get this done. My next stop—the petting zoo." She hooked him an eyebrow full of questioning cooperation.

He picked up his pace like a suitable, albeit slightly brooding, assistant. "You do the bunnies. I want the tortoises again."

The smile she fought probably came off more like a grimace, as he had an affinity with the plodding residents of the tortoise enclosure. "You know, Julius Caesar, that Rome wasn't built in a day, so you don't have to stack the tortoises up three deep while you're feeding them."

"I'm just laying some groundwork that I might build off of later with my gymnastics, that's all."

When he shrugged his shoulders, she noticed the extra bulk they were gaining from his exercise routine around the crow's nest. "Are you excited to get your equipment tomorrow?"

The cart stalled on a wad of gum, and he lent a hand to push through it. "Yeah, and to see my folks. Wish they could stay longer but mom's leading a class for teacher certification credit, so she can't miss. You're planning to hang with us, right? I'd like them to spend some time getting to know you."

A black alpaca startled as they came up the walkway, probably feeling guilty for stretching its long neck between fence strands to procure a bite of fresh grass. Maybe she'd have Dory walk the alpaca on a lead line over by the hay meadow to let it get its fill. "I want to, really. It will be good to get my thoughts off of this place for a day or two."

She heard several thumps on the concrete wall of the tortoise enclosure and knew his fan club had already begun gravitating over. There went his unmistakable charisma again, even with an audience of hump-backed melon eaters. "I brought in a couple of cantaloupes for them today." When he smacked his lips together, she tried not to focus on them, but the power of suggestion was far too strong.

"You're such a pushover for these cute tortoises," he replied. "So, I'm not the only one with a soft spot for the hard shells."

She laughed and slung a pad of hay to the alpaca as the bunnies scattered from the motion. "I'm guilty of having a few soft spots." She pulled the top off the bunny food mixture first. Next, she divided up the veggie mix and sprinkled it around the enclosure so even the shyest rabbits could have ready access. Tortoise shells clicked together next door, and she glanced over to see if Brace busied himself with paving the Roman Road again. He was. "Brace Cordan," she said, her tone laced with authority.

He stepped over a body length and gained a new stack of turtles—all open-mouthed. "Does the name 'Capitol Merger Bank' mean anything to you?"

Out of left field, the pitch barely missed her headband. She shook her head in a total dodge.

"It came up on Marty's computer when I logged in to get the Wi-Fi operational. All I read was the subject line."

"That's not our regular bank, likely spam mail trying to snag some business."

"Oh, it already had some business of ours, or Marty's, to be more precise." He fed the tortoises and stepped to the rim to catch some of the extreme slow movers with the core of romaine lettuce. "The subject line read 'transfer completed.' Do you think he might have put the clouded leopard payment in another account for some reason?"

"I doubt it. I don't usually look at that kind of thing until the end of the month. He lets me check the accounts receivable behind him to catch any errors before payroll comes through again." Finding a shady spot, she threw a sealed tub of carrot sticks beside the pen for Dory to sell to the adoring public.

"Cerise is providing me the daily gate receipts for my marketing records, but I'm sure you're already getting those."

Her throat tightened at his assumption, as Marty had always documented that portion of the accounting. She'd never really thought to check behind him. Unease settled on her chest, an unthinkable reaction for a woman standing in a pit of bunnies. "How about I ask you to show me at closing time and we not worry about it until then? We've got a beautiful day to enjoy in a little slice of heaven, so let's not fret."

He dropped the last of the lettuce and stepped into her area, causing the rabbits to dart away in fear. "Weren't those the famous last words of the little Dutch boy with his thumb in the dike?" he quipped, placing a finger under her chin to make her face him.

"A catastrophic flood is definitely lurking," she replied with all sincerity. "We call it the Shakespeare Festival. And this year, I even get to embarrass myself with dancing in front of the faceless crowd."

"Tell yourself they'll all be looking at me, O-Jell-o the amazing aerialist, and not at you, swirly-girl-on-the-ground."

"Thanks, Brace. You're really helping me cope." She broke from his magnetism and headed back to the food cart.

He lifted his palms up like it was the least he could do. The reactive bunnies skedaddled in a hundred directions.

She needed to flee also, as the primate wing was calling to her for animal care duty. Maybe the baby Schmidt's guenon would allow her to cradle it next to her troubled heart, if it could give up its fleece blanket long enough. What was she holding onto for security?

As if on cue, Brace bounded out of the petting zoo and picked her up off her feet in a bear hug, complete with simulated growl. "Ah, Desdemona, how awful to love thee only to leave thee to insufferable demise," he quoted with brash vigor.

She laughed with his therapy, feeling the evidence that his weight training was coming along nicely. "At least thou came in love, poor O-Jell-o—and not some less noble quest." She enjoyed their closeness until her feet found the pavement.

His sparkling eyes spoke one message, but his muscular arms held her at a distance as if parting wasn't such sweet sorrow from his perspective. He blinked and the look disappeared, replaced by friendship and camaraderie.

She gave him a showmanship smile and took the food cart in one hand, even though he refused to relinquish the other. She tugged it, so he came closer one more time.

"Love *is* the most noble quest," he said in a hushed voice.

When he kissed her knuckles, Paisley gave Desdemona a little more credit. He released her hand, but now she wasn't so sure she wanted it back. Having two hands would make holding the guenon baby easier, plus give her dancing some symmetry. In a compromise, she agreed to keep it for now, but stay ready to lend it back to him, should he ask for it. In the meantime, she'd try not to get ahead of herself emotionally, as he'd only given her a few hugs and a couple of smoky lingering looks. A level-headed girl shouldn't read between the lines, but then a forthright man wouldn't lead her to, either.

"Guess this is where I get off." Brace pointed toward the aviary.

She'd been in such a dreamy state, she hadn't realized they had arrived. Crackers fluttered at the cage wall as she pushed the food cart by. "There's my baby now," she cooed, scratching the air as though to pet the pet bird.

"Ah, Iago, thou traitor," he replied, clutching his heart as he disappeared for duty.

"Thine nectar pitcher sittith under the bar," she added, waving him off on departure. What she wouldn't wave off was the sensation from those arms of iron that had held her like she was something precious. No, she would keep that with her and dream about it for awhile, at least while the visitation remained sparse. For a Saturday, that wouldn't be long, at least, not long enough. She sighed. For the first time in her adult life, her commitment to duty waffled.

Chapter 12

Brace walked back to the parking lot, feasting his eyes on Pawnee Rock with his arms wedged between his mother and father. The sun slipped further down on the horizon, ending the most remarkable day. Leta and Paisley had treated them to a picnic in the backyard after he'd gotten the rings rigged up in the aviary with his dad's help. The pommel horse ended up in the petting zoo area, giving the alpaca something new to covet. His Cornhusker cohorts fell in step behind him, making Paisley laugh at their antics which only pulled his smile wider.

This must be what it feels like to be free, he thought, glancing at the aqua bands starting to form along the horizon. His ticket to freedom rode in his father's shirt pocket—the first payment on his student loan debt. Closure of the loop would come with a hand-delivery tomorrow, but his heart seemed satisfied that it was out of his hands. Great, maybe that would make room for something else. Paisley laughed again and it pleased him deep inside. *Affection has sensitive ears to hear what it wants.* He wanted to hear her.

The farewell became protracted with lots of promises, including their return late summer to take Weston and Riley back into the land of Cornhuskers in time for the start of fall semester. Paisley hugged his mother goodbye and tolerated her straightening a wisp of fly-away hair. The handshake his dad pressed on him felt signatory, and for the first time the blessing of honoring his father and mother truly meant something to him. Their truck soon pushed into the distance and the prairie grasses waved goodbye. When they returned to the bonfire, Travis and Chloe had joined the group, making it a perfect time to address the festival.

"Now taking bids for anyone wanting to perform with us in the Shakespeare Festival in two weeks," Brace said, his eyes roaming the group.

Mimi jumped to her feet like a kid. "Ace, you know I do," she replied in an overtly familiar tone.

Kurtis shot him a look and he shook his head like he didn't have a clue.

"Count me in for the duet on Lemur Island and maybe something else, too. I haven't even seen the wildlife park up close, as I stayed mainly outside when Re-Occupy camped here."

"Good point, Mimi," he conceded. "Let's plan to have an on-site brainstorming session on Tuesday afternoon, say around four. We can do a little improvised practicing and see how it's coming together. Anybody ever do any tech work for sound systems?" Weston raised his hand and Brace pointed back at him. That got a nod of commitment and he clapped.

"Food service?" Paisley asked next. "We're thinking about floating some food carts near the performance venues. Anyone want that type of involvement?"

Riley knelt from the circling log seating and flipped his hand toward the fire. "I work the food concession at the football stadium for my work study job. Guess I could handle that position. What kind of stuff would I be hawking?"

"Jigglers for the O-Jell-o venue." Brace waggled his tongue back and forth.

"My brother's in the Great Bend Optimist Club," Travis volunteered. "I heard him talking about a new cotton candy machine they recently bought."

Paisley stifled a laugh beside him and he had to know what was behind it. Knitting his brow, he gave her a stern look and watched the fire dance over her fair features.

"I've always thought the mandrill's backside looked like a cotton candy creation," she said with a teasing look. Chloe promptly lost her composure, eliciting the most delightful laugh which caught like wildfire around the circle.

"Honey, I've just got to see that," Mimi said. "If that don't make me want to sing, I'll be a monkey's aunt. Everything doesn't have to be all Shakespeare-like, does it?"

"Not at all, we can mix it up to keep the show fresh," Paisley replied.

"Well, I may not be able to hide my crazy if some critter has a cotton candy tush," Mimi admitted with a grin that showed off the gap between her front teeth.

"We have an opening in the kangaroo enclosure," Paisley said. "We like to have the public walk through while music is playing. We've used strolling minstrels in there before."

"Travis and I want to do something together," Chloe

said, her shoulder nudging into his. Travis took her hand with a loving look. "He plays harmonica and I want to accompany him on the flute. Would that make a good mix for the kangaroos, Paisley?"

The fire popped and a fleck of ember shot toward the rim. Kurtis kicked it back with his boot which earned him a hand on his arm. Mimi started looking cozy beside the big guy and Brace sensed God's favor weighing on the whole group.

"Perfect," she replied. "I can get a loaner from my neighbor Jacey if you need the flute." Chloe nodded and leaned into Travis who rewarded her with a kiss on the forehead.

Brace noticed that Paisley dropped her gaze and wondered what she was avoiding. "We may need a reader for some of the Shakespeare stuff," he suggested, trying to finish up the recruiting. "Our gatekeeper Cerise recites from memory. She's working on the balcony scene from 'Romeo and Juliet' but we still need someone to be the object of her affection, so to speak. Any guy willing to stand in that role?"

"Depends on what she looks like," Les quipped. Lars didn't laugh though, and when the heckling died down, he anteed up for the job.

Brace couldn't hide his pleasure. "You know, since I'm ruining Othello's name in my skit, you're welcome to corrupt Romeo accordingly."

Kurtis gave a belated snicker and Brace pointed to him for the idea. "I have a fabulous vintage front bumper in my garage if you want to go as Chromeo."

"That's sharp, dude. I like it a lot," Lars said. "Chromeo, Chromeo—where for art thou, Chromeo?" The quote set the ring afire with laughter with Kurtis proving loudest of all.

"It'd be truly awesome if the bumper was the rail on Juliet's balcony," Mimi shared, "and she polished it the whole scene while he crooned his love up at her." When she started buffing out a spot just above Kurtis' kneecap, he seemed to relish the treatment.

"That's classic, Mimi," Paisley replied. "The audience would adore it. And we could give him some animals wandering around his feet."

"Not the tortoises. That's my territory," Brace said, staking his claim under no uncertain terms. He'd already been training those moveable building blocks and fully planned to use them.

"How about the bunnies then? We could run the scenes side-to-side so the audience won't have to relocate again."

"Perfect—except for the unspoken connotation of love and the rapid, uh, reproductive tendency of bunny rabbits," Lars said, visibly uncomfortable with the subject.

"That would be part of the joke, a little innuendo for the adults, and cute little fur balls for the kids to enjoy," Brace explained, shooting a look to Paisley for her approval. She nodded and he clapped his hands. "Looks like we're done, except Les doesn't have a specific job."

"Let me float for now, and I'll be ready to hop into something if it comes up Tuesday," Les replied.

Paisley stood and brushed the bark off her back pockets. "And with that final bunny joke, I'm going up on the rooftop to get some dance practice in."

Thinking that might give him the opportunity alone with her he needed, Brace started to stand as well. She gave his shoulder a little push and he instantly had to retract the idea.

Kurtis chuckled as Mimi scooted even closer to him.

"You know we all want to come up and stargaze from the roof when it gets darker," he reminded her, trying to veil the intrusion it represented. That might not have worked.

"Give me about twenty minutes then," she conceded, refusing to look at him directly. She had no more started up the path than company appeared by bicycle. When the rider unfolded, the unmistakable frame of their pastor approached.

Steve tossed his helmet into the grass. "Mind if I crash the party with a quick thought I'd like to share?"

"Go ahead, Pastor," Brace replied. "The fire's all yours." A word from God would feel good about now anyway, as part of his flame had just been snuffed out by the departing dancer. Steve stepped across the log and settled into Paisley's old spot, his knees doubling up toward his chin. Brace guessed that the lanky man wasn't much of a dancer, though athletes often had skills hiding behind their apparent agility. He'd keep that in mind if they fell short of talent.

"I wanted to encourage each of you to look for God's purpose while you're here with us," Steve said. Several heads nodded around the group, as the fire died back in increments. "I hope you've experienced the blessing of our community reaching out to you. That certainly doesn't come with a requirement to pay it back, but you can always find a way to pay it forward."

"Like the basketball clinic," Les replied, taking an immediate high five from his brother.

"Yes, the twins and I have decided to hold a ball-handling clinic the week after next. That gives us time to get Vacation Bible School cleared off the calendar this coming week."

"Both sound great," Brace replied, his marketing mind working on overtime. "Maybe we should find a way for both groups to visit the wildlife park. We could extend a group rate and you could ask the parents for it up front, as part of the clinic's fee. That second week would be especially perfect, as we'd need to hold our dress rehearsal that Friday. You could invite the parents to come early for pick-up and join the kids in the park."

"See? This is the type of enrichment I'm talking about," Steve replied. "Reach out to the community with your special gifts and touch someone in a divine way."

"Wow, I might have to up my game in the 'Chromeo and Juliet' skit," Lars lamented. "I planned to just read the lines, but Juliet—I mean Cerise—is memorizing hers."

"Practice together in the afternoon after VBS," Steve suggested. "Iron sharpens iron. You'll be amazed at what you can accomplish when you do it as unto the Lord."

The wisdom hit home with Brace as Kurtis murmured "amen" down the way.

"That's my word for the evening, ladies and gents. Thanks for sharing your bonfire with me. Now I'm off to some outstanding mulberry cobbler that my lovely wife has whipped up."

"We bid thee adieu, good parson," Brace said, speaking in an Old English accent. Steve stood and made some ridiculous hand gesture and exited with a flourish, scooping his helmet as he went. Brace thought about running up the hill to attack the pavilion and take his plunder, but he knew enough time hadn't gone by yet. Waiting wasn't his forte.

"Maybe I could pray over our group for a few minutes," Kurtis said in the lull.

Nodding, he closed his eyes but could still see the languishing flames flashing across his minds-eye. He hoped the fire was the only thing dying, as he just had to get up that hill.

"Father, we ask you to be with every decision we make for the festival, bless our new friendships, Lord, and let us walk in obedience to your will. Help us share our talents with the surrounding community, and we thank you for the Re-Occupy reinforcements. Amen."

A springbok wouldn't have gotten the jump he delivered, as his feet hit the pathway up to the pavilion. Brace could see a figure dancing in a fevered pitch on the roof. He felt the pull of destiny hoisting him uphill, so he determined to make it count.

~

Paisley went through the Desdemona sequence again with fawning swirls and graceful bowing at her pretend husband. Sudden changes of direction came next, as unfounded accusations were hurled her way, and then a peaceful transpiring with fluid motion, ever downward into the smothering scene. What a way to go, she thought, pulling long breaths to fuel her burning lungs. They matched her aching thighs, as she needed to improve her conditioning if the lunges were to be held anytime at all. She bowed and let one leg slip in front of the other, sending her into a set of splits that would eventually lead to marshmallow pummeling.

Down below she spied the bonfire, glimpsing its

glow as she twirled by the south railing. Her thoughts shifted to Brace, and a familiar confusion swept over her. Something burned there she didn't know how to extinguish, even if she'd wanted to. The feeling seemed to increase every time they were together, fanned by his iron-armed hugs that made her knees go weak. When she added the sensation of touching his soft wavy hair and glimpsing those sparkling blue eyes, her mind shut down to autopilot. Was that because love resided somewhere else, not in the brain?

She stretched out her calves by stepping onto the rimming bench and waited for the tautness to yield. Lights from vehicles along the highway twinkled back at her. No resentment followed them this time. *Is contentment a state of mind?* She switched calves to complete her cool-down stretches. Whether that could translate to a satisfied sense of place was another matter. Brace was searching for a home base to settle into, yet she still fought the urge to venture forth. How the twain would meet proved too mysterious to resolve, especially with her overload of commitments at work. The dancing added yet another layer of responsibility, but she employed it to personify her quest to be a body in motion.

Sounds from the stairwell told her the dance session had to wrap up. Before she could dash away from Iago's betrayal one more time, a pair of feet floated above the top step.

Brace emerged, walking inverted up the spiral rail in a handstand.

She clapped at his theatrics and fanned her neck, hoping to generate some coolness in the still of the evening.

He shoved off with a handspring and stuck the landing.

Now she had to share the rooftop and suddenly felt too winded for conversation. "Too exhausted to talk," she managed, lowering onto the bench. She'd rest but possibly not extend an invitation to him, as she was uncertain how she felt right now with all the go-versus-stay ramifications running through her mind.

He turned in her direction and hesitated a few seconds, raising his arms parallel to the roof. "Didn't come up here to talk," he replied, sureness leveling his words. He crouched at the knees and then like a springboard, popped into a flip and landed a little closer to her.

Tracing the bulk of his musculature in the dimness of night, her eyes feasted while her heart held back. "Go ahead, get your workout in, too." She drew a breath and leaned back against the wood, the weathered grain rough against her bare skin where the tank top looped low. A faint breeze swept by. She knotted the shirttail higher to let her midriff breathe.

"Maybe I will," he replied vacantly, and off he went in a series of round-offs that made him appear to be in flight.

The fluidity of his movement tugged at her heart. She knew she had to look away or she'd be a goner.

A string of cartwheels brought him back into admiring orbit like the rising moon. He blew out the exertion and drew a slow breath, then inverted his body in a handstand at the top of the stairwell.

"You're floating tonight." She swallowed but found no resolution for her tenseness.

He swung out of the handstand and planted right in

front of her. "I'm free," he claimed, rotating his shoulders like shirking some invisible weight off. In one fell swoop, his arms circled down and encased her, making her stand up before she could resist. "And I'm celebrating." He held his distance.

All she could see was his muted outline surrounded by a host of shining pinpricks of light. If she was still alive, she wasn't breathing anymore. By some miracle, she managed to wet her lips as he closed the distance between them, tightening his hold as he came closer.

As if bowing for prayer, his face moved past hers until their cheeks eventually brushed. His breath caught in her ear, and an electric arc of goose bumps tore down her arm. He trembled like he battled to maintain balance and withdrew ever so slightly, his stubble pulling against her cheek, like flint striking a trail of fire. An aqueous quench came as his lips slid over hers, dousing her doubts and filling her with weightless delight. The outpouring of affection repeated after a rapture-filled breath, and the next quelling effort lasted more than a lingering moment. Finally, his lips moved to her forehead. She clasped the hills of his muscle-bound shoulders, exploring by fingertip up into his wavy hair.

"My swirly-girl," he whispered, nosing into her bangs.

She buried her face in the crook of his neck, and the sensation was not unlike suffocating. And maybe part of her was actually dying—the part destined to wander. Tears came to her eyes. "Hold me right here."

Somewhere in the fragile duration of their embrace, a sway caught faint rhythm and Brace led her through it without loosening his grip even a fraction. Standing atop a rock, she was now being held by one. "Thank God for you," she whispered onto his skin. He winced from the touch but recovered, keeping his rhythm as he cradled her in his arms. Her restlessness vanished into the blur of night.

"Can we come up? The stars are out," Kurtis called.

She giggled as a final hug tightened around her shoulders. He released her for the group to share the platform, always the gentleman. At the first pang of separation, his hand slid into hers and knocked the sensation away. When the others arrived, they weren't the only ones holding hands.

Chapter 13

Their day off turned into a gypsy migration, but Brace found merriment in the company and delighted that his Re-Occupy friends mixed so well with the Pawnee locals. Unsure how two rock formations would hold their interest for very long, he'd mostly come along for the companionship and the sense of adventure. These were rocks the Indians had played on, so who knew what sat on them before that? His curiosity piqued, he studied the road map one more time. Paisley glanced over and gave him a smile, while Les and Lars debated the finer points of European basketball from the back seat. Memorizing the distance between the two sites, he closed the road atlas and leaned back in air conditioned comfort so Kansas could woo him.

"Here we are, arriving at Stop Number One, Mushroom Rocks State Park," Paisley soon announced. She nosed the car off the road.

Easily the tiniest parking lot he'd ever seen, Brace quickly took inventory of the area. The park contained a two-compartment restroom, an interpretive sign by the trail head, and eleven empty parking spaces. Kurtis pulled his truck in beside them with a lurch. That left ten empty spaces.

He pulled his hat off the dashboard and opened the car door. "Onto the wilderness," he charged, finding it quite pleasant to stand again. Gravel crunched under his feet as he wandered toward the sign. He'd read until their little group collected, and then push them up the trail of stratigraphic intrigue. The outhouse door squawked behind him and he realized the reconnoiter would be temporarily postponed. All the more time to read through the natural history detailed on the sign.

"This is going to be so fun," Mimi said, popping a pink hat over the disparity of her dye job.

The effect tickled his eyes so he patted her head like a poodle.

Kurtis walked up and mumbled through the sign introduction and the phrase "Dakota sandstone" seemed familiar. "Oh, I've got the camera," he mentioned. "Thought it would be a fun place for some pictures. Sorry Chloe wasn't up to coming out today."

"Travis had to work anyway," he replied. "She can save up her energy for our practice tomorrow. We likely won't get our day off next week, as the performance will be too close. I'll double check that with Paisley to be sure, though." Weston and Riley walked up, hats in place and ready to scout the trail. Les and Lars brought Paisley along with them. They were all finally present and accounted for.

"These are Dakota sandstone, just like Pawnee Rock," Brace said.

Paisley tied her shoelace on the fence railing and gave him a sideways look. "I think the mushroom caps are concretions. You know, something that was included within the sandstone."

He studied the short trail and something loomed directly up ahead. When she took a limber step or two ahead of him, he determined to fix that. "Fellas, this is the smallest state park in Kansas, so let's get to the rock formation without further adieu." His voice rose with the challenge and then he broke into an all-out run. He soon flew by Paisley with ease.

Kurtis took a few heavy-set jogging steps in response.

"Hey, no fair," Mimi replied, getting left behind in her sequined sneakers.

Footsteps came up behind him and he figured one of the twins was giving him a run for his money. He kicked his stride into higher gear as the foot path narrowed through a meadow. The first rock tower came fully into view and the oddity of it blew him away. Again, the footsteps closed in on him, so he had to keep his lightning pace up even though his calves were killing him.

"First touch wins," Paisley called, shouldering by him with a longer stride.

He started to protest at the thought of being outrun by a girl, even if it was his swirly-girl. "R-r-r-rock me," he growled, finding some added speed to muster up to the formation. He nudged past her with three steps to go, which made him slam up to the mushroom stem with unfortunate force. He grunted and threw himself onto the shady side, gasping for air.

She grabbed her knees in recovery and breathed heavy into the morning air as the rest of the group caught up. When Kurtis slipped the camera out of his pocket to immortalize the moment, Brace had just enough time to lift a victorious fist over Paisley's hunched frame with the mushroom rock standing sentinel over them.

"This is so out-of-this-world cool," Mimi said, tucking a few loose hairs under her hat. "Look, this low one has a peephole. We've simply got to get a shot of that."

"I agree. Everybody get up there," Kurtis replied, pointing to a double concretion that sat half-shaded by a willow tree.

Brace bounded up the backside of the cracked gray blob and studied a hole the diameter of a small child's torso. "How about men on top and Mimi in the peephole?" he suggested as Kurtis found the best angle down below. "Man, this texture is so…granular."

"Heavy ground mass is what makes it so resistant to erosion," Les clarified, pulling up on the upper platform. "That's why it got left behind. The sign said something about an inland sea."

"Right, Kansas was under a midcontinent ocean at one point," Paisley added. "Where do you want me, Brace?"

He teasingly held his arms open and laughed, then pointed down front where the concretion leveled into a lower platform.

She shimmied up next to the peephole and Mimi wiggled into position.

Kurtis looked through the camera and glanced up on the rock. "You guys up top need to do something to give this pose more character."

"Tip your hat with your left hand," Brace said. Hats went airborne down the line.

"Now stand on your right leg and bring your left knee waist-high," Lars added. He caught his gymnast's balance and made the pose, though the slight slope of the upper platform made it a little tricky.

"Now everybody smile," Weston added, anchoring the far end.

Kurtis snapped the picture and started walking around back to join them on the rock.

Brace hopped to the lower level and squeezed Paisley in a belated hug.

Kurtis found Mimi still occupying the hole and took a cheesecake photo of her close-up.

Recognizing the attraction, an idea came to Brace. "Let me take one of you two," he insisted, motioning for the camera. Kurtis smiled and handed it over, hustling to get in the shot.

"Go up top and hang down toward her," Paisley said. "That will be an extraordinary pose for such an out-of-the-ordinary place."

"And a not-so-ordinary couple," squeaked Mimi, batting her eyes like an Egyptian princess. Kurtis tried to kneel but couldn't get low enough, so he laid flat on his belly and extended his hands down to frame out the hole. Mimi reached out and their hands clasped.

Brace focused the camera and the lens soon clicked closed. "Awesome, dude. You're going to love this shot." Paisley leaned in to catch a glimpse in the monitor and giggled at their antics.

"We're going to try to climb up the tall one next," Riley announced. A mass migration headed for the adjoining formation as he grabbed for Paisley's arm to help her down. Kurtis extracted Mimi from the hole and lowered her over the edge safely to the ground. Pausing in the willow's shade, he pulled Paisley back to him for a private moment.

"So what did I win from our little race?" he asked, testing her receptivity.

She looked down at the rock face as two dimples appeared on her cheeks. "Maybe you'll get a treat at Rock City," she hinted. "This park is small and our space is limited…"

He touched her chin and her eyes warmed a bit, enough that he had a new reason to look forward to their next stop.

"There are a few more mushrooms across the access road to see, and that's about it."

"More concretions on Dakota Sandstone." He spoke slowly, like the words held some secret enticement.

She took the camera from him barely brushing his hand. "Just like our Pawnee Rock."

The inference wasn't lost on him. A sudden surge of energy had to find an outlet. He jumped down from the rock, and ran toward the human totem pole attempting to climb the taller formation.

"Give me a hand up, Weston," he insisted as Kurtis strained under the twins' weight. In seconds he was flying, his feet finding Les' shoulders and his hands landing on the vaulted mushroom cap. He pulled himself up and turned to lock arms with Les. "Send Mimi up next."

"Golly, Ace. I don't think so," she replied, as the camera slipped into her hand. "Let's get one of you and Paisley."

He saw his favorite dancer examine the man-linked route and wasn't sure she'd opt for the climb. "Paisley St. James, come to me, babe." He beckoned and she stepped into position, placing a hand on Weston's shoulder. "Easy up," he said, a bit nervous to watch.

Poised and balanced, she came to him one human ladder link at a time.

Once on Les' back, he reached for her. His shoulders brought him what he wanted and his chivalry kept him from kissing the daylights out of her, right there atop the mushroom rock in front of everyone. The space seemed to open up around them like they'd been teed up on the open prairie, paired together in the great wide open.

"Hold a pose now," Mimi called from down below.

He leaned backed against her and crossed his arms, satisfaction streaming from his heart. She shouldered against him, running an arm through his and they locked elbows right before Mimi flexed and lowered the camera. "Shoot the human bridge, too."

"Better hurry, darlin'," Kurtis warned, his back starting to sway. In a matter of moments, Les leapt back and crashed to the ground, soon followed by his mirror image. Kurtis fell back against the mushroom stem and Mimi ran over to lend him some personal assistance.

Brace couldn't see anything more from his upper perch, but thoughts of how to get down started to plague him. He could seat-drop Paisley into the catch basin of Weston and Riley's arms, but that left him to freefall on his own. *The dilemma of every up was the down it eventually required.* At least he'd have gravity working for him. Kurtis moaned and he figured Mimi was using some shoulder-rubbing TLC on the big guy. Magnetism proved just as bad as gravity and had the same effect, if you were heading downward. And he sure needed down.

~

Paisley could see Rock City bump out from the horizon as the car made a wide curve. Humps of concretions broke the ground in a scattered field of what looked like a giant bocce ball game left weathering on the lawn for centuries.

Brace whistled at the scenery. "Get a load of that." He sat transfixed by the concretion array.

"We've gotta climb each and every one of those," Lars insisted.

She caught the high five of her backseat passengers as she glanced in the rearview mirror to spot Kurtis and the rest of the gang. She pulled into a grassy parking lot, braked, and took the car out of gear. When she cut the ignition, it stirred the explosive energy of its occupants.

"Rock City, here we come," Brace said, winking at her before pummeling the door panel with his shoulder. What ensued looked like a manic attack on inert matter, as each man set himself against the bulbous rock. She met Mimi in front of a cute stone hut and fished her wallet out to place an admission donation into the self-service box.

"Guess if you could build a ball pit for grown men, this would be it," Mimi teased.

Folding the dollar wad through the donation slot, Paisley chuckled and turned to find the savages she'd delivered. The guys were already atop the closest boulder, giving Kurtis a hand up. "Should we join them or stay on the ground?"

"I'm only good for the lower rocks," Mimi replied. "Maybe I can sweet talk Kurtis out of the camera and be the photojournalist for the rest of the afternoon."

"I believe you could sweet talk Kurtis out of anything, Mimi. He's a childhood friend, but I've never seen him turn into putty like this."

"Great. I'll take that as a compliment because…I'm feeling it, too." She gave a little mouse squeak and wrinkled up her nose. "We need to practice more, get our harmony down, so to speak. That should make for some heart-to-heart time together, at least in the afternoons."

"Good plan. Hey, let's walk under the boulders they're climbing so we can be there if anybody needs first aid. Thank goodness most of these are at ground level, so I won't have to go vaulting off into thin air again."

"Yeah, I like to walk up and walk down on my own two feet."

"Same here. I hope Brace doesn't call me up again, as I've had my flight of fancy and I'm done going aerial."

"You two look like you're working on something… special," Mimi added, finding the first partially buried concretion with her foot.

Paisley led the way higher up, wondering how much to admit to a new friend who'd known Brace longer than she had.

"You know, Ace never hooked up with anyone in Re-Occupy. Didn't look like he was interested…in a girlfriend, that is. He was plenty interested in the issues, though. His passion clearly flared in that arena."

"Scripture says there's a time for everything. I think I met Brace at a crossroads of time."

"A real God thing," Mimi added. "He needed a job…and maybe a little female attention. You've given him both, and look at him now. He's never been happier."

"What about Re-Occupy, Mimi? Are you going to miss it?" She came back down the sloped rock face and found the ground much more suitable. A pink hat soon appeared at her side.

"Being a part of Re-Occupy was like living inside a mirage. We all knew it wasn't real life. We could see real life everywhere we went. I don't blame Brace for dropping out when the election went against him. Leland couldn't have lasted long, so it was just as well the water thing happened in Dodge City. I…I'm glad I got to come back to Pawnee Rock. And I get to sing."

"Yes, you do—and we need you, too." She admitted. Brace whistled and motioned her over to a side fence where a metal cutout of a cowboy reclined. "See you in a bit." She jogged over to see what the commotion was about. The tree overhead seemed to be dripping something luscious. "Mulberries!"

He had a funny expression on his face. "Yum-yum. This is what I want for winning the race at Mushroom Rock."

"I have to pick your berries?" She slipped a playful smile into one cheek.

"And feed them to me one at a time," he added. His eyes sparkled at the concept.

She tugged off a rather large specimen and dangled it from her fingertips to start the mandatory feast.

"Oh, no," he replied, insistent on having things his way. He picked a berry and wedged it between her lips, holding a finger up to keep it in place. Closing the space between them, he nibbled the berry out by brushing her lips with his.

Instant pleasure flushed her senses. "Come back here behind the tree." She hooked a berry-stained finger through his belt loop, more than willing to privately serve his reward.

Chapter 14

Walking into the primate wing brought a heady satisfaction with it. Brace shouldered down the trail beside the twins. Paisley had stopped to adjust a feeding tray on the outer wall of the Colobus monkeys and jogged toward him to catch up. Kurtis looked pretty cozy beside Mimi, discussing their Lemur Island number. He paused to collect the group so Paisley could share her ideas about a Shakespearian monkey act. Movement caught the corner of his eye and someone gasped, making Weston and Riley shy back.

Mimi pulled on Kurtis' arm. "Oh-oh-oh, I'm mesmerized by this character."

A large animal circled to the front of its cage as if cued by her attention and the cotton-candy fur feature came their way, rear-and-center. Brace honestly had to overcome a touch of being appalled at the critter's over-the-top markings, both facial and furbearing, and then realized why it might appeal to Mimi's vaudeville taste.

"That's Juno, our mandrill," Paisley replied. "I'm afraid you're looking at every bit of showmanship he's got, Mimi. He spent overtime in costuming and no time perfecting his stage allure. All he does is pace the pen, around and around."

Mimi squatted and grabbed the wire mesh, transfixed on the animal.

Worried that something half-baked might emerge from Mimi's creative vault, Brace telegraphed a concerned look toward Paisley.

"My dance takes place right over here," she said, "with the Schmidt's and DeBrazza's guenon. I plan to use the pass-through tunnel and go into both cages."

"Did you decide on 'A Midsummer Night's Dream?'" he asked, hoping to forestall Mimi's distraction. Weston started beckoning to a baby monkey dragging a fleece blanket, and the critter came willingly to him inside the wire mesh.

"No, we did that play a couple of years ago and I wanted the show to be different to draw a larger crowd," she replied. "I've chosen 'The Tempest,' and I'm dancing the part of Miranda around my little island plagued with magical spells."

"Help yourself to the row boat hull in my garage for the shipwreck," Kurtis added. "And what if we play 'Come On Down, Miranda' for your soundtrack? We can get a CD set-up, because I'm going to be way too busy."

"Over here—singing with me," Mimi said with certainty.

Brace didn't want to hear whatever came next, as they barely had the resources to pull off what had already been planned. Defensively, he put his hands over his ears and combed through his overgrown hair. Everyone shifted back toward the mandrill as it made another round, face-streaked with cosmetic appeal and rear end poufy with decoration extraordinaire.

Mimi placed her hands on her hips. "Picture this—I start out a medley with a fast-paced 'Hide Your Crazy' number in heavy makeup to match the mandrill. Next, I downshift to something a little less zany, like I'm sizing it up, but I'm singing with Kurtis on guitar, still trying to figure it out..."

"We could do 'I Don't Want Easy I Want Crazy' to tie in with the first song," Kurtis replied.

Brace caught the hint of a smile on Paisley's face and decided to keep mum and let this creative collaboration run its course. Then he'd rein it back into the corral, if necessary.

Mimi's hands began to whip the air, circling in opposite directions like she was pulling the thought into her realm. She must have hit invisible pay dirt as a light bulb came on in her expression. She grabbed Kurtis by the arm and squealed in delight.

Brace translated the sound as train wreck imminent and gnashed his teeth.

"I end with the slow song 'You Make it Easy, Easy,'" Mimi added, "which begins with frenetic crazy and ends with critter-under-control as I stroll the mandrill around the cage, capturing him under my spell."

Kurtis started to clap but decided to hoist her in the air instead, making Mimi squeal with delight. The mandrill actually stopped pacing and regarded her as she came back down as though the critter-kook attraction had already started.

"I don't know, Mimi," Brace said, attempting to diffuse the overloaded act.

"Let's give this some thought," Paisley replied, a

finger on her chin. "Since we're trying to perform in a grouping to keep the audience from having to move so much, this might actually be a good idea. All they'd have to do is turn their chairs around. Plus, you'd be singing, but I'd be dancing. That lends some balance."

"See, Ace," Mimi replied. "We could add this medley of mayhem to balance the Shakespeare stuff. Really, I have a good feeling about this."

"And what if we gave the kids in the audience an opportunity for face painting?" Chloe asked. "I've run that booth before. It wouldn't be hard to do."

"And we could add a little girl dance troupe out front here for the high-spirited first number," Paisley added. "Leta could help me make little pastel tutus, so the girls would also match the mandrill. I could ask Jacey next door."

Wide-eyed, Mimi gasped and virtually started jumping up and down like a kid.

It occurred to Brace that the act lent itself to girly and he slid a mocking smile to Kurtis who was in too deep to extract himself. The big guy never looked happier.

"Don't forget my brother-in-law's cotton candy machine," Travis said, walking up to the group in his identifying uniform, grease-streaked from the auto shop. Chloe fluttered over to greet him like a butterfly.

Her hug made Brace wish he'd been standing closer to Paisley. "How's all this going to segue into your Shakespeare number?" he asked, turning his attention to the primate performer.

Biting her lip, she turned and examined the double cage like she'd never seen it before.

"I can help make it work, sound-wise," Weston

assured him. "I think Paisley's number will be more classical and less whimsy. So maybe she's the one who needs the little dancers."

"Oh, I have my little troupe," she assured him, motioning to the monkeys poised above on the branches. "This will be the island of my captivity…and I'll fall for my Ferdinand right here in its confines."

"Lucky Ferdinand," Brace quipped before he could stop the words. Heat encircled his collar as his friends laughed at him justifiably.

"I'll take the offer of the boat, but no Ferdinand, please," she said. "The story ends like a dream, with the actors melting into thin air, so I'd rather have my beau imagined than staged. That way I can play to the audience with my dance."

"I'm definitely front row then," Brace replied, hopelessly hooked on her, dance or no dance.

"Let's hit the kangaroo courtyard next," Travis said. "Chloe and I have come up with something we think you'll like."

"Lead on, Trav. I want to hear it." Brace reached for Paisley as the group migrated on toward the next great idea. Mimi chattered against Kurtis' rapt attention as Weston stooped to check power supply points for the sound system along the way. They'd have to devote themselves to lots of practice to pull this off, but momentum held an upswing and he'd draft up on the current.

"We need to coordinate Desdemona's dance with O-Jell-o's gymnastic moves," Paisley said over his shoulder.

He drew her closer and couldn't think of anything else he'd rather do than hover over her dancing form with his power iron-man act from the rings. "Thou twisteth my arm, Desdemona," he replied in his smoothest voice, "to do the very thing I dreameth." The look she gave him through her eyelashes made him want to add the vault so he could fly without ropes. An unleashing of gymnastic ability was in order. He hoped his shoulders would be ready.

~

Having the Vacation Bible School finale at the wildlife park turned out to be a true stroke of genius, Paisley admitted, standing at the pavilion's perimeter to restrict trash exodus. She'd managed to talk Marty into reduced family passes that included feedings at all stations, giving Amyl his biggest day at the grill since Independence Day. Brace sat in the far corner, laughing it up with Pastor Steve and his basketball entourage. Next week they'd repeat the same deal with the basketball camp, which she'd heard was topping out at thirty kids. Not bad for such short notice, mainly because Steve seemed to be an instant draw with his former NBA career.

If she really wanted to give credit where it was due, she'd be hanging the upswing on the Re-Occupy members. New ideas seemed to flow into the community with them. What started out as a small-town effort to help the downtrodden now seemed to possess flipside benefits. Recognizing God at work in her community, Paisley let humble receptivity trickle through her. If God was at work, she certainly didn't want to miss the blessing. Brace's laugh skipped across the murmur of the pavilion's occupants, drawing her gaze toward him.

He represented a blessing of a different kind—

companionship. As much as she'd tried to remain mere friends, something more than friendship played at her heartstrings. Right when she'd doubted if anything more would come of it than a few possessive hugs, he'd kissed her up on the pavilion roof.

Pawnee Rock always elevated her into the presence of God, up high and away from earthly bothers. So what did it mean to have Brace seal his intent right up there under the watchful eye of God Almighty? Afraid to answer, she began walking around the pavilion's edge, smiling at the Bible school participants as she passed. When she paused at Pastor Steve, he immediately turned his attention to her.

"We've had six children place their faith in Jesus as VBS closed," he said. "I remember you told me that's when you came to Christ as a kid."

The spiritual warmth returned and lightness came over her. "Yes, that's right Steve, the summer between fifth and sixth grade. I still remember walking home afterward, talking to God through the treetops to make sure he knew I was serious." She rolled her eyes thinking about it now, as God knew everyone's heart. No proof was ever necessary with him.

"I'm opening the baptism pool to anyone else who wants to join us this Sunday," Steve said, searching the Re-Occupy group for takers. "If anyone wants to identify with their Savior through believer's baptism, just let me know." He stood to rejoin the church folks, a commanding figure amid the munchkins he cared so much about.

"Add me, Steve," Brace said, locking his eyes on the pastor's face. "I trusted Jesus as my Savior in high school, but never followed through with baptism. It's high time I did."

"Okay, Brace. Plan to meet me behind the choir room at the end of service. Bring a towel and be prepared to share some of your testimony."

"You sure you want to give him an open microphone?" Kurtis teased, his face joy-filled.

Paisley glanced between the three of them, wondering what in the world God was up to.

~

The sanctuary seemed to fill up behind them as Brace sat shoulder-to-shoulder with his Re-Occupy friends. Kurtis had come down and joined them after the opening worship session, capping Mimi on the end of the pew and squeezing everyone else into too small a space. When Paisley responded to a plea from the pulpit for more nursery help, he begrudgingly let her pass. Her absence left him able to sit back with more room, but also generated an empty space he could hardly define.

His sensitivity about spiritual calling somehow got all tangled up in his emotions for her. What a quandary to hash through on the eve of his baptism. He glanced down the row and saw that Travis openly held Chloe, making his affections clear to his home church and God. Would he be willing to man up like that after he got his personal business straight with God?

Steve took the stage and gave his sermon-in-a-sentence, referring to living a deeper life. Although he mentioned at the outset he'd be targeting the children from Vacation Bible School who'd accepted God's gift of salvation, the pastor assured the entire congregation there would be wisdom enough for all to have a take-away from the message. As Steve extracted his challenge over five areas of living, Brace wondered if his vagabond group could relate. Most of them were on the run from something. His run would have likely continued had it not been for his student loan payment coming due. Fortunately for him, it served as the chokehold he needed.

Kurtis soon returned to the front for the closing song, which cued him to depart for the choir room area. By the time he bypassed the legs of his comrades, Paisley stood waiting in the aisle opposite the altar. Somehow, as he gave her a meaningful look, they didn't seem to be in two different directions. Paisley stood in the same direction God was beckoning him. He'd return to that revelation at a later time. Right now, he had a dousing to attend. Trailing six half-pints into the back, he placed a hand on his chest and eyed the large wooden cross over the piano.

In the men's robe room, he shucked his Sunday attire for gym shorts and a T-shirt. Watching from an angle across the rear of the pulpit, he witnessed the junior members of the baptism party walk in and be dunked. One by one, they came up gasping for air. The last one in, he held his breath. A peace descended on him as he waited. Finally, Steve flashed him the thumbs' up signal and he took an intentional step toward God. His ankles were wet before he knew it and Steve reached for him with his NBA grasp, like a work of Michelangelo crossing the breadth of the Sistine Chapel.

"Of course, we're finished with the VBS converts," Steve mused, forgetting to transition to his next candidate.

Brace waded deeper in the pool, the cool waters inviting him to a memorable experience. He knew the congregation must be laughing, but couldn't hear it with his focus on God. He only heard the water lapping at the stairs as he advanced a few more strides. He'd been on the move all his adult life. Funny it should come to a standstill in chest-deep water under the shadow of the cross. When Steve nodded for him to share his testimony, the words that came weren't the ones he'd been practicing.

"Today, I hear God calling me for a closer walk with him. I trusted Jesus as my Savior back in high school. And I committed myself to that decision as Christ committed himself to me. We've been a partnership-in-motion since then. But there comes a day of reckoning where a wanderer has to stop dragging the Holy Spirit around with him in the trivial pursuits of this world, and surrender in obedience to something deeper—if I can borrow Steve's term." The pastor nodded, and he skimmed the surface of the stilling water with his fingertips as he crossed his hands over his heart like he'd been instructed.

"Today I relinquish my need to wander, as I feel the Spirit telling me that I've finally found a home. I need God in my life and want to identify with him through this baptism. I want him to lead me from now on, and I'll follow in obedience." Steve took his hands as he glanced at the cross one last time, then sealed his eyes for the plunge. The water came mercifully, over his shoulders and around his head until all the world was blocked out except the incredible feeling of God-inside-him. The hydrous burial lasted long enough for him to plant it indelibly in his mind, and his clothes hugged his skin upon emergence.

"Wait!" a man's voice called, halting him as he

turned toward the steps with the pastor by his side. The church fell quiet as one individual took his stand to make things right with God. "I want what Brace has, permission to stop the wandering as a lost man." Pushing through the water to the front glass, Brace looked out and saw his roommate from the crow's nest. His heart moved with compassion and he beckoned Weston forward, keeping his arms held high as if to welcome anyone else. Steve rejoined him and pointed to the microphone at the pulpit, centered and ready for confession.

"I'm sick and tired of shallow living," Weston said. "I want more. I want God and all the blessings he has for me—beyond what he's already given me by bringing me here, which is considerable." His voice broke and he stood away from the podium. Brace looked out and Riley was approaching the front in sharp strides.

Steve beckoned Weston back to the pool area from the right door and the two roommates shook hands on the platform steps. A soft hallelujah made its way to where he stood back in God's waters and it made the experience all the more remarkable. Time stood still while Riley collected himself.

"The love in this community has changed me forever," Riley said. "At first I didn't realize it was God working through you guys. But now my eyes are opened. As soon as Brace said something about being a wanderer, I knew deep inside my heart that Jesus was calling me out. Today I step toward God, and I'm happier than words can tell. I believe in Jesus and I want to be baptized, too."

A surge bolted through his spirit and Brace felt like

he might fly right out of the baptism pool. Steve motioned him to the far side of the tank and he crossed his hands over his heart, this time to subdue the beating beneath. Weston appeared barefoot and apprehensive, descending down the steps to become a man of God. It was a noble brotherhood the three of them would share for the rest of their lives. Immersed and sealed—without the wander.

Chapter 15

Paisley pulled at the burgundy dance dress that Brace had selected for her Desdemona outfit, bringing its generous scooped neckline back up onto the round of her shoulders. A week filled with backdrop rigging and prop acquisition now blurred in her memory as the Friday crowd leaked into the park for entertaining. One way or the other, they would certainly be amused, even though only the petting zoo segment had been designed to be funny. Well, that also possibly included O-Jell-o, depending on the birds and the gelatin-slurping minions.

She fought off her annoyance at Marty for dumping the job of clearing cash from the token machines on Brace at the last minute. Instead, she searched for Amyl only to find him releasing Riley with the gelatin jigglers food cart. He would need a few minutes to work the crowd before she would signal to Brace and his crew. Checking the aviary interior, she spotted Crackers-turned-Iago, the betrayer. She wouldn't hold the pending betrayal against her favorite feathered friend, not in the least. Cerise stepped up in similar costume, hers the lime color of hickory nut husks in the fall.

"Ease into position and start in about three," she said. The gatekeeper nodded, swirling the back of her dress as she circled the crowd. As practiced, she would dance a circuit through the aviary as the introductory narration progressed, and then yield to the general's entrance. That sequencing freed her up to shepherd the junior actors on their way into the slurp-fest. She would pass Brace on his way to the rings and curtsey in flat-footed submission, like a good little Desdemona, trying not to think about how he hadn't touched her since the day of his baptism.

Pushing into the door of the aviary, she spied the boys behind the serving counter. Brace's shoulders appeared over the washing station counter by the exit. Good, she wouldn't have to mix words with him, as they both knew what they had to do.

Cerise began with a clear voice and explained their comedic interpretation for the jealous tragedy of Othello. Upon hearing her stage name, Paisley slipped through the plastic curtain, bowing and dipping her arms while she turned the fluid circles of a woman filled with love. She stopped to admire one of the bare-branched bird perches where silk flowers had been wired into place, touching one delicately.

Completing the loop, she had just started a spin when Crackers tried to alight on her shoulder. The bird aborted the touch-and-go and she passed by Brace with a flush on her face. His white-stretched gymnastics costume couldn't hide his musculature and his shoulders carved out twin hillsides bulging from the tank top straps. No great wonder the birds flocked to him.

Ducking behind the safety of the plastic curtain, she took several breaths and felt a small hand slip into hers. Little Cade joined her, barely able to stand still as Brace leapt to claim the rings dangling from the aviary frame. She knelt to be companionable and the rest of the daycare kids soon joined them to catch the real star of the show. Brace inverted his body with steady control and launched into the most incredible routine of turns and twists, maneuvering the rings at his whim. She recognized the iron cross as he held the position, noticing his neck veins bulging in strain for the first time.

Ever so slowly, Brace rotated horizontal and stayed.

As she held her breath, Crackers fluttered and led the rest of the birds, to the exaggerated oohs and ahs of the crowd. Time stood still as Brace hovered in his bird perch role. At long last, he eased his legs toward the ground and dropped. Half the birds stayed put until he stood fully erect. The audience exploded into applause. Exchanging a smile with Cade, she counted to five and shoed the boys out to consort with their general while Cerise unwrapped the next portion of the fated plot.

Stepping back toward the exit, she pushed the feast cart out into the aviary, keeping behind the curtain. Brace took a few pompous steps toward the table and lifted the dome off the platter to reveal blocks of gelatin for the slurp-fest. When he bowed toward his men, a wink swept her way. She pulled at her burgundy costume, feeling the reactive heat of his masculine attention.

Laughter erupted as the audience fully enjoyed the boyish antics of the shared feast. The distraction provided her the opportunity to sneak a hand beyond the curtain with a cup of nectar. Crackers came first and she clipped the lace hanky to his leg, then brushed him back inside. Brace made a game of the boys apprehending the token of betrayal and it became a fine romp of possession. Only when he offered the nectar cup did Iago relinquish the hanky, which Brace dislodged with practiced ease. Cerise told the tale of the ill-planted talisman and Brace played the betrayed husband, launching out into a series of angry round-offs. The boys scuttled back offstage into the foyer and she took her place by the exit curtain. Brace landed up front and held in a push-up position. Several of the larger birds flew onto his back.

She swirled into the scene in nonchalant gaiety and nestled up front, kneeling next to him. As if repulsed, he jerked away, sending the birds to wing in his outburst. Back to the rings, he put together his final combination, eventually lowering himself toward her as she reclined directly beneath his midair position.

"Mulberry," he whispered.

She startled into action. They hadn't rehearsed this part, only that he would give her a cue to come to him. The birds arrived before she did, flaming his back in color and feathered hush.

He bent and tugged something from his shirt with his mouth.

When she glanced up, a beautiful pale rose blushed with apricot waited for her, his final gesture. She took it, unable to avoid Brace's gaze as his message of love became crystal clear. Lowering to Desdemona's fate, she encircled her loose hair with her arms, forming a trap for the marshmallows soon to be delivered by his rowdy minions. The kids reappeared as her world turned fluffy white, and she heard Brace exit the rings and moan into the lacy hankie. When Cerise capped the scene with a summation about jealous desserts, the crowd quickly demonstrated its appreciation for the performance. The boys came back to center stage laughing, digging her out of the marshmallow pile and holding hands for their final bow.

Adjusting the costume to maintain her modesty, Paisley caught a glimpse at how flushed her chest had turned and knew it hadn't been from the dancing exertion. Embarrassed at having made the private exchange in such a public venue, her knees gave in to the impulse to flee. Through the plastic curtain and out the entrance door she flew, Desdemona-on-the-run. Only once did she think about the possibility of having a bird on her shoulder. Too late now to care about the animals, she had to outrun apprehension and still make her next venue.

~

Brace settled in behind the paying crowd as action was scheduled to begin down the primate wing. Lemur Island had turned pretty farcical as the "Madagascar" tune hit home with the kids in the audience and they all rollicked together for some good clean fun. Kurtis wasn't half bad, but the addition of Mimi carried the show. Now he felt somewhat out on a limb, but from the rate little girls were having their faces painted, this mandrill number could be a big hit. Weston clicked the microphone for a sound check and nodded to Kurtis. Chloe finished her last customer at the face-painting booth and released her to the front row. Things looked ready to go.

Mimi appeared and he choked when he saw how

163

much make-up she had put on her face. Once she climbed into the mandrill's cage, though, he could see a family resemblance and understood her approach. Her opening lyrics about cutting her bangs with scissors reminded how sorely he needed a haircut. Maybe Leta could do it tonight between the two days of festival performance. He scanned the crowd, but couldn't find Paisley anywhere.

The first time the chorus cut in, a group of tutu-wearing girls leapt up to flank Mimi, though they stayed outside the enclosure. Thinking one girl had been left behind, he studied the individual more closely and found it to be the object of his desire. With butterflies painted on her cheeks, she looked fifteen years younger. The song "Hide Your Crazy" echoed from the performers as the girls tilted their heads to make their ponytails waggle to fit the bill.

Mimi looked a little rascally back there striding back and forth, but she'd always been borderline saucy. He chuckled as the song progressed and it seemed like she was chasing the mandrill, which persisted in doing its one trick of circling the premises. Predictable animal behavior with a side car of fun music, maybe it had the makings of a classic.

Chloe knelt at the screen and took a few shots with her phone camera as the cotton-candy-in-motion girls popped back up to carry through the chorus one last time. Paisley gathered the pint-sized dancers and Kurtis stood, strumming his guitar through the bridge into the next song. Mimi's lyrics now claimed she didn't want easy, she wanted crazy. He thought she'd be in luck with that request, though the mandrill's dour expression made that outcome seem iffy.

Kurtis echoed back a line or two and Mimi gave him a wrinkled-nose grin that must have teased him up a notch. At one point, Mimi tracked the mandrill and Kurtis tracked her. The whole parade came off too doggone funny. Chloe took a picture of that action, which Brace thought might be cleverly reproducible for drumming up business.

Mimi exited the cage while Kurtis led her into the final song with an instrumental introduction. She strolled by the front of the cage, shaking hands with her dancer-girls including Paisley. The frilly stuff under her skirt tipped when she bent over like a teacup trying to pour. Boy, she looked like that mandrill coming and going. How'd she do that? His wonderment only added to his enjoyment of the number. Brace hoped the crowd liked it, too.

"You make it easy, easy for me," crooned Mimi, stroking the wire enclosure as the mandrill passed. She sang her next line to Kurtis who had slipped off the stool to stand with her against the wire. The whole thing was a mesmerizing moment and Mimi's honey-laced alto held everyone spellbound. She tugged on a prop and entered the cage, meeting the mandrill face to face and softening her voice. Kurtis grabbed for the microphone and freed her hands as she whispered the last lines to the critter. Then she uncoiled a rolled fruit treat and the mandrill accepted one end, nibbling it while Mimi tugged it forward. In the end, the two-tone singer got what she wanted, as the mandrill followed her like a shadow, having turned putty in her hands.

Paisley started the applause and Chloe got several final shots as Mimi turned and winked at the crowd. She dared to pet its head and got a short rub on it before the fruit treat was finished and the animal reverted to wild, slinking to the back of the enclosure. Laughing with her face hidden in her hands, she had the presence of mind to take a tippy bow as the audience hooted with pleasure and applauded. When Kurtis joined her for a second bow, the crowd extended its ovation.

Chairs scraped and the venue turned one hundred and eighty degrees to catch the next act. Paisley tiptoed by, her costume now a series of red and yellow flames rippling off one shoulder. He managed to wrap his hands around her waist as she passed, even though it occurred to him that those who played with fire got burned. At the moment, he'd venture to take that risk.

Entering the double guenon compound, Paisley wiped the butterflies away, smearing the paint across her cheekbones which left him to wonder whether the scuffing had been intentional or not. Several of the monkeys shifted positions as Paisley tucked herself into the bow of Kurtis' rowboat that had keeled over on its side in the front corner. Several seconds ticked by as Weston engaged the CD and a classic rock song rose like a phoenix over the show.

"Ladies and Gentlemen, presenting Shakespeare's 'The Tempest,'" Cerise announced.

Paisley rolled out in a tumble and stood, wary of the surrounds as the haunting music bid Miranda to come on down. She leapt toward the cowering guenons and split the family units apart like bowling pins. The audience gave a collective gasp until the baby swung down into her arms as rehearsed. A preschool boy up front cheered and his mother grabbed him in a similar hold. She slid a set of fairy wings onto the baby and ferried it off to work its magic while she swirled around the cage assessing her island prison. Her jagged skirt hem flounced with her turns, catching Brace under the sternum with something akin to heartburn.

The baby monkey approached the alpha male and he tried to pluck its wings off, but had to settle for tasting them in place. Drawn by her fairy, Miranda singled the male out and blew a cloud of pixie dust at him, turning the air purple. With a face-wipe, the male left its perch, so the dancer followed with a few spins.

As she drew back with her legs extended in muscle-fueled lunges, Brace found himself losing the storyline in deference to her movement. Athletic and graceful at the same time, she had him totally captivated. The crowd sat quiet.

Escaping through the connector tunnel, Miranda slipped into the DeBrazza's guenon side of the enclosure to continue her island search. Every one of the inquisitive monkeys came off the upper ledge and followed her around. A juvenile jumped onto a trapeze swing and she pushed him away in rejection—which it seemed to enjoy.

Brace leaned on the cage's corner. When his rings came to mind, he wondered if he'd react the same way to her push back. If it helped him eventually catch the dancing flame, he sure would.

The troupe of primates shadowed Paisley to the escape chute and she slammed down the barrier before they could join her with the Schmidt's clan next door. As the music hit its crescendo, she beckoned to the alpha male and it came to her in full monkey swagger with the baby fairy riding its back. Miranda took them both and ended the routine by kicking the shipwrecked boat back to floating position, setting the male inside, and freeing the baby fairy to romp on the island's tire swing.

A drumming sequence punctuated the song's end as Miranda dropped to her knees to shove the boat off the shore with her Ferdinand. She threw one arm up to signal the end and her gaze caught near the cage's corner. Applause thundered from the crowd.

Moved to connect, Brace could barely feel the wire as his fingers entwined the strands reaching out to her. When she touched him from inside the primate cage, the fire became his.

"Please join us next in the children's petting zoo for comedy-in-action," Cerise said.

Knowing he had to outrun the crowd, Brace straightened and reluctantly released the dancer from his grip and his gaze. For now, he'd cut up with his tortoise building blocks, but he'd find his way back to her somehow.

Taking a shortcut behind the albino alligator tent, he raced for the bunny park and soon found Edgar, the camel rider, standing by the black alpaca with a tux T-shirt on complete with a red satin bowtie. Still dressed in his white gymnastics costume, Brace hadn't given the first thought to slapstick accessories. When Edgar produced a pink sequined headband, he stretched it between his hands and attempted to plant it somewhere inert. The thing landed around his right thigh and stuck, so he left it to ride out his tortoise act. He stroked the back of a black bunny as the crowd ambled up to catch the show.

Cerise chose a quiet moment to introduce the comedian who gave her a cheesy wink and took center stage. Edgar introduced the animals around the petting zoo, cracking personality jokes about various ones and suggesting orthodontics for the alpaca. He told his hard-to-pull-one-over-on-the-tortoise joke and Brace inverted into a handstand in the middle of the herd. As the topic drifted off to the bunnies, he offered a few carrot sticks to get his tortoise buddies stacked up like he needed them. Edgar broke the bunny punch line and kids from Steve's basketball clinic laughed like hyenas.

A comical question about a tortoise and a bridge came next, leading Brace to step off a distance from the compound. With a final glance at the stack, Brace launched into a series of round-offs, tucking his arms around his knees to sail over the turtle hurdle. He landed perfectly, but sand caused his right foot to slip, so he stretched the momentum into the splits. A tortoise lumbered up and nipped at the sequined headband on his thigh. The kids lost it again.

Edgar seemed to be wrapping up his act, so Brace extracted himself from the compound and tried to slink away by the honey badger cage to dust off. A giggle announced that he had company. He caught sight of the flame-woman approaching behind a bush as he wiped tortoise admiration off his dress whites. Her fingers dug under the headband and pulled it off his thigh, insisting to have it freed by his ankle. Quick to oblige, he brought her closer to have a word.

"Sit with me for 'Romeo and Juliet,'" he said, his throat too dry for lengthy rapport. He glanced up, and Cerise was already leaning out of her chrome-trimmed balcony. Lars appeared from a nearby service room dressed in gold tights with a carburetor filter for a shirt collar in modified Elizabethan style. Now Brace had to chuckle, as the most liberal poetic license stood poised on the verge of transpiring.

Paisley sat off the tortoise side of the bunny pit and he landed beside her, pulling her over until little space remained between them. When she dropped the pink headband into his lap, he mouthed his silent thanks with deliberate delivery. Lars stepped beneath the balcony and the laughs began before the dialogue started. His arm found Paisley's waist and she didn't object.

"What headlight through yonder showroom window breaks?" Lars asked. "It is east Detroit…and Juliet is the sunroof. Arise fair deluxe options package and kill the envious base model. It is my Chevy—oh, it is my love." Lars stepped forward like a jointed tin soldier, craning to accentuate his neckwear.

Paisley's snickers weakened Brace's resolve to remain neutral. He wanted more than anything to absorb the love deflected in the scene. With Paisley so close, how hard could that be?

"Chromeo, Chromeo. Where for art thou, Chromeo?" Cerise buffed out a pretend blemish on the bumper while delivering her inquiry. "Deny thy dealership and refuse thy vanity plate, or if thou wilt not, I shall no longer be a convertible."

The laugh started at Brace's waist and bubbled up, too loud for proper gentlemanly behavior. Playing the comedy coward, Paisley fought hers off, tucking into his shoulder to muffle it. He'd lost a bit of composure, but at least they were together.

"Oh, wilt thou leave my service record so unsatisfied?" Lars asked, fingering his neck.

"What service satisfaction canst thou have tonight?" Cerise paused her buffing and leaned out.

"Perhaps an oil change," Lars suggested with a quick

check of his arm pits.

Brace was in laugh-snorting tears now. Hopes of squelching his merriment failed to be an option. At long last, Paisley buckled over his thighs in breath-stealing laughter.

"And possibly, the exchange of thy model's faithful vow for mine." Cerise fought for control up in her perch, as the bunnies ran hither and yon around Lars and his mechanic's approach to romance.

When he spotted the actress on the verge of giggling, he drew a breath. If Cerise lost it, Brace wasn't sure he could salvage himself. Good thing he'd sat out this act.

"But—I gavest thee my voucher before thou didst even request it." Cerise leaned further over the chrome bumper to deliver the surety of her trust directly. She shook the shop rag at him and tightened her upper lip to hold her composure together. "Oh, that I couldst double your coupon's value, to give it yet again." She threw the rag and it landed on his filter neck-piece as Lars botched the catch.

He sniffed it and pressed the rag to his heart. "Oh, blessed Bondo night," Lars uttered. "I am fearful, though. Being it prime time, that this be nothing but a commercial promotion—too sweet to be anything more than a sale-a-thon dream."

"Young Juliet?" Edgar called in his falsetto nursemaid voice. "Comest thou inside now."

Brace pointed out his location to Paisley and her cheek touched his finger as she shifted.

"A thousand times goodnight," Cerise bade, tossing him a kiss with both sets of fingertips. "And your warranty—may it reach one-hundred thousand miles, my love." She disappeared below the chrome bumper, but Lars stood moonstruck by the tossed kiss and lingered in the moment with the rag upon his cheek.

Brace raked his chin and Paisley looked over at him.

"Parting is such sweet sorrow," Lars quoted in rigid delivery. Then he sniffed at the rag again, deep in thought. "Perchance, we'll make this pit stop again one day soon—and I shall claim the title of her heart. Fare thee well, lords and ladies. Until that day, fare thee well."

"Be mine," Brace whispered, his heart orbiting into conjunction with Paisley's fond glance. The audience roared its approval of the spoof act all around them, but he only had eyes and ears for her. No response of love followed, nothing at all.

Chapter 16

Excusing her inability to give Brace a response on her busyness to wrap up the festival's first run-through, Paisley held the gate open for guests and allowed the parade to stroll through their last feature. The kangaroo compound had been dressed up with quotes from the Bard that Cerise had printed out in script font and affixed onto wooden dowels.

Travis and Chloe now sat centered in the cusp of the arching trail on bar stools of alternate heights. The last guest traveled through the portal and she allowed the safety spring to pull the door closed. Les stood inside the gate with a cart stacked with tiny hay bundles, handing them out to the children in the group. She turned and noticed the exhibit sign had been altered to read "Shakespeare's Court of Love."

A harmonica sounded on the afternoon wind and it seemed like the farewell signal of a departing steam engine. She'd always held the harmonica to be a peppy type of instrument, but Travis pulled his breath through it steady and slow, releasing a different emotion. Before the engine pulled completely away from the station,

Chloe's flute piped into the accompaniment like a butterfly on its smokestack. Paisley didn't recognize the song, but the disparity between the two parts proved captivating. When it came to an end, the scattered families clapped their approval, causing the kangaroos to shuffle about to the delight of several toddlers.

When the flute began the ascending first line of "Where is Love?" Paisley felt Brace's presence behind her for the first time. Not pressing or demanding, he simply stood nearby so they could share the experience. Elevated by the simple clarity of the flute, her awareness ramped to high alert. As the harmonica played back to the flute, her heart began to yearn in response to his possessive request. Her hands folded behind her back involuntarily, and his warm fingertips played on her palms, tenderly insisting on a clasping grip.

At work and in full sight of the public, she dared not pursue further contact. But they both heard the quest for love and answered it together with a singular touch. The flute's music rose ever higher, and she felt certain the treetops would part and release it to heaven, but the notes trailed off leaving only the drone of cicadas to haunt her thoughts.

Travis led off with a downbeat version of "You Can't Hurry Love" and Chloe finished playing out each line. The effect came off similar to the way old married couples finished each other's sentences, comfortable and expected. Would she ever know someone that predictably? And was that someone Brace? His thumb traced the lifeline on her palm, and she soon joined Mimi in the crazy girl department.

Kurtis appeared on the far side of the exit gate and

she gave him a nod for door duty. Mimi walked up seconds later with a tube of lipstick in her fingers. Not that she needed more embellishment. When Kurtis turned to welcome her, Paisley saw a smear of mandrill make-up on his cheek. Well now, maybe love could be hurried after all, as they'd only known each other two weeks. Chloe played her last flourish on the flute and the insects took over the concert once again. Travis thanked everyone for coming out and invited them to linger as long as they wanted. Her hands emptied and Brace vaulted over the gate before she could lament his absence.

Steve had approached the instrumentalists and placed a hand on Travis' shoulder. When Brace walked up, he got similar treatment. The men seemed to shine under his encouragement.

Paisley marveled at what strength a positive Christian influence lent. Hearing Mimi laugh at a guest's flattery for her performance earlier, her thoughts turned to her oldest animal handling friend. Maybe Kurtis needed some positive influence too. She wandered over and pulled the exit gate from his competent grip.

"Why don't you go join the boys' club in there?" she suggested, nodding toward Steve. "Mimi and I can get this."

Kurtis didn't hesitate to take her up on the offer as Weston and Riley came into the compound through the other gate. It fell together as a real convergence of the mighty men of valor when Les shoved the hay cart aside and was followed by his brother, Lars. Chloe opted out of the testosterone huddle and came toward her with a knowing smile on her face.

"Dating lecture one-o-one now in progress." She tucked Jacey's flute case to her side to exit. Mimi drew an unsteady breath and straightened her blouse subconsciously, pressing her red lips together in sudden concentration. Standing nearby, Chloe hung her head.

Since Paisley had been fighting the attraction battle too, she thought a word of empathy might be in order. "Steve requires accountability among the men in our church." She opened the gate for a satisfied family of five. A little girl with angel wings on her cheeks skipped out and asked to be carried to the car. She recognized the replication of Chloe's neck tattoo and had to smile. The power of influence surrounded the locals at every turn.

"Does accountability require confession?" Mimi asked, wincing a bit. Her gaze flew to Kurtis, and the gentle giant stood round-shouldered beside Steve, wiping at his cheek.

"Probably—but that's only a guess. Women receive support of a more nurturing sort. The men are held in higher account, as they are the leaders of the family unit. Steve wants them to be strong and courageous as they serve the Lord—and as they live their everyday lives."

"Kurtis makes me go weak in the knees," Mimi replied. "He's more than special to me."

"Then treat him special—like a mighty man of God," she countered. "If he survives Steve's scrutiny, that is."

"I'll try to hold back," Mimi promised lamely, sticking her pinky between her lips.

Paisley reflected on how Shakespeare frequently dramatized the volatility between a man and a woman in his plays. The struggle was universal. She could attest to that.

"I've never met anybody quite like Travis, so ready to listen and give encouragement," Chloe said. "He doesn't mind me leaning on him. He's strong that way."

"We all seem to be falling under the same spell," Paisley said. "Shakespeare wrote 'let virtue be as wax and melt in its own fire,' but I don't think that's a God-honoring way to approach falling in love. We have to maintain a pure heart, and let it lead the way. Then we can try to pray before our lips follow up on the emotional surge part."

"Now that I can do," Mimi replied, setting her jaw as she peered at the man huddle. "He gets me with his music, you know. It comes in my ears and filters right through my heart."

"That's his spiritual gift, Mimi, endowed by the Holy Spirit to return praise to God. Make sure you don't turn it into his Achilles heel."

The singer tilted her head in contemplation. "What about you and Ace? Is it his baby blues that get to you?" Mimi batted her lashes to accentuate the guess. Chloe giggled and started to blush.

Paisley grew uncomfortable trying to hang words on what she was beginning to feel for him. A glance inside the kangaroo court helped her remember. "Let's say it's his charisma-in-motion," she replied. "More like a package deal, his movement is convincing, which becomes spellbinding at times, but definitely magnetic."

Mimi gave a little clap under her chin and would have probably hugged her had the gate not needed opening for the next family to exit.

Little Cade ran up to her and clasped her legs. When

she gave him a pat on the head, he flashed up an unrestrained smile. "Brace was absolutely great today, wasn't he Paisley?"

"Yes, fantabulous," she agreed, ruffling his hair. "Remember to be here again tomorrow at nine-thirty, just for half an hour to get your part of the morning show in."

"Of course, I've got to be here," he argued. "Brace can't do the gelatin-slurp fest without his minions—and that includes me!" His mother pealed him off her legs and insisted the boy depart with the rest of the family.

She gave a little wave and looked over at Mimi and Chloe. "See? That's why the men have to have the accountability, because the next generation of mighty men of valor is watching from the wings."

Mimi's mouth gaped open and popped closed when Kurtis laughed, the huddle breaking up. "Here comes charisma-in-motion now." The singer's tone seemed much more subdued. She gave a little wink and walked ahead, anticipating Kurtis coming up the path. Travis cut in and swept Chloe away.

Brace turned toward her as if he'd caught a hint of their meaning. She blushed as she pulled the exit gate open.

Steve passed by first and gave her a round of applause. "Great show, Paisley," he offered, letting his kiddos scamper through. "Between the ball-handling camp and this festival, I'm worn slam out. Must be my age speaking for me, because you know I'm typically young-at-heart."

"And in bed by nine-thirty," his wife added. She led their youngest out and laced her hand through his elbow, making the most of the walk back to the van.

"Thanks for coming, pastor," Paisley replied.

"And for including the wildlife park in your camp fee," Brace added. "I don't think Shakespeare and basketball make traditional court partners."

"Well maybe they should," he responded, pulling his wife to his side. Brace looked at Paisley and lifted his brow, attempting to captivate her with his nuance. He bent over the closed gate and held her in suspense for a few seconds as a maverick kangaroo passed by the portal.

"I have two words to say to you, Desdemona," he revealed.

"I'm sorry?" Her thoughts skipped to the jilted outcome of the O-Jell-o plot.

"Token machines," he replied, rocking an invisible target with his hands.

"Goodness me, I totally forgot my promise to show you how. That would have landed us in the doghouse with Marty, for sure. Come on out, my Moor-man, and let's get to the deed."

"Ah, I like it when you take charge like that," he replied, exiting the compound.

She smirked and fidgeted with her dance wrap so he wouldn't try to hold hands. When he popped the headband over her eyes, her vision went pink. Now he needed to take the lead and he did, with a velvety touch on her palm.

~

There might have been a better way to bring the token money back in to the office but the animal food cart stood ready and willing, so Brace had mustered its services. Now piles of change ran down its trays like lava. Paisley backed into the office door and helped leverage the cart over the threshold so they could get it inside and secure the money in the office vault. She reached into a cabinet and pulled out a handful of bank deposit bags, tossing them on the desk.

"What now?" he asked. "Marty didn't say anything about counting."

"No, he does that and the bank has an automatic change counter to verify the deposit amount. Let's get it bagged and in the vault. I'm starving for some odd reason."

He frowned and grabbed the closest bag, throwing fists full of coins through its zippered opening. "This is ludicrous. Marty should be here right now, not us. You're hungry because you skipped lunch, Paisley. We have two performances tomorrow. You can't afford to let your energy level slip because you're carrying too much of his managerial load."

"We're a small operation, Brace. That means special events bring extra work along with the hubbub. But we need the fundraising aspect, so we give a little more of ourselves…"

"Everybody but Marty, it seems." He slung a coin bag against the vault door.

"My grandma used to say 'if something's not going right, figure out a better way.' Well, sometimes I dream things would be different here—more like how we're doing this year's festival, with creativity outside the box."

"And Marty liked all our ideas, but he wouldn't pay an extra dime to get us the help we needed." He reached for a bag marked 'dimes' and shoved a mixed load into it. The gesture felt retaliatory, as it left Marty some work to do. Good.

"He's a skinflint, through and through. Maybe you should talk to him. Try to get him to see the future of this park, instead of trying to constrain us with status quo."

He threw another sealed bag against the vault door and tried to navigate through his burgeoning anger. The room grew quiet except for the Midas murmur of coinage being rough-handled. When the door exploded open, he almost threw a handful of silver across the desk.

Kurtis held Chloe's cell phone out like it had turned radioactive. "Thought you guys might want to know about this." Mimi shadowed her duet partner and Travis pulled Chloe inside the office. Brace held his hands up like he refused to kowtow to the money, so Paisley rushed to finish the task solo.

"I posted the mandrill performance on YouTube," Chloe said, her plucked brow arching. "I figured it couldn't hurt to get it out there—it seemed so unusual."

"Good idea, Chloe. A solid marketing move," Brace replied. As Kurtis squared the display around for him to view it, he scanned the image trying to judge whether it would do more harm than good. Paisley busied herself with the vault as they huddled around the tiny screen.

"It's gone viral," Kurtis added, his words hanging in the air.

Paisley rose slowly and her chin tipped his shoulder, so he raised the phone for her to take a look.

Brace grew uncertain of what to expect. "How many hits?"

"Just walking the phone in here from the parking lot, it went from twenty-five hundred to five thousand," Kurtis replied.

Brace glanced at the far wall and tried to perform a mental calculation, though Mimi's giggles were distracting. "Can we post another sequence? Pick one from O-Jell-o with Paisley dancing under my iron cross. Add an invitation to a special Sunday matinee at five, perfect for a date destination. Can you manage that, Chloe?" Paisley made a faint noise as if to object, but he had to move on this or lose the opportunity. They'd worked too hard not to reach their extended audience. "This is just what Paisley and I were talking about, expanding our tent flaps. So here we go."

"I need to video someone announcing the invitation for Sunday," Chloe replied, taking the phone back.

Brace scanned the tight group, all potential candidates and highly capable."Use Mimi. That will tie the two clips together. Viewers will recognize her from the mandrill's cage. What other footage do you have?"

"There's a segment from 'The Tempest' when the monkey gets in the boat… and Les shot a piece of our instrumental duet that includes kangaroos at our feet."

"Use part of it all—just enough to get the viewer interested, and then trail with the invitation," Brace added. "I'd like to have consensus. Are you guys with me on the encore showing?"

"Count on me," Kurtis replied without hesitation.

"That includes me," Mimi followed. Travis nodded and grabbed Chloe's wrist as she giggled her endorsement and hooked Mimi with her wink. Kurtis trailed out behind them leaving a very silent Paisley packing up the food cart.

He stepped around to the handle and gave the cart a tiny push to get her attention.

Paisley looked up and fear claimed her features.

"Marty's going to be furious if this is anything but a huge success." Embedding several smaller plastic tubs inside a larger container, she busied her hands to offset the shadowy threat of recrimination.

He placed his ring-calloused palm over her nurturing hand and made her stop fidgeting. Their eyes met and he stood his ground, confident of the decision. "Let it be on me then, not you." He tapped his chest with his free hand. "I'm the fall guy for Sunday. You're simply my fateful accomplice, Desdemona. Now…let's get you some dinner." She opened her mouth as if to object, but he tipped his head like he'd hear nothing of it.

They would hold an encore performance accessible by patrons further out and maybe skyrocket his escalator clause past the fifty percent mark. That would do the old student loan payment some good, and save him a little interest in the long run. If only he could hold his troupe together, which might take more than an elastic pink headband.

Chapter 17

Lemur Island had been surrounded by a crescent of lawn chairs as the afternoon performance of the Shakespeare Festival sat poised to begin. Static came over Paisley's radio and she triggered the response lever to speak. "Go ahead," she said as Brace walked up to her expectantly. She held up a finger and squinted, trying to hear the message.

"Make that two charter buses, now pulling into the parking lot..."

"It's Cerise calling from the front gate. It looks like we've got some late arrivers. Stall Kurtis, will you?" Brace turned and gave a shout to the singer, flashing him a five-minute signal.

"The bus marquee reads Dodge City, but I don't have reservations."

"Dodge City, Brace," she repeated. "Who could that be?"

"Sam Granger," he replied, breaking into a run. "I'll head them this way. Tell Kurtis not to start until we're back here with the whole group."

"Roger that," she replied. She cued the radio and

surveyed the crowd. "Brace is coming up there, Cerise. Try to get a head count and we can settle up later to expedite things."

"I'll shut the gate behind them," Cerise replied.

When the air waves went silent, Paisley knew some crowd control would be in order. She stepped around a cluster of family members on a quilt and made her way to the bridge. Kurtis came back off the island and met her there between gates. "Late arrivers are on their way down, a Dodge City group. Brace thought they might be led by Sam Granger, whoever he is."

"The stockyard manager," Kurtis replied, a smile curling his lips. "The guy who covered the Re-Occupy hospital bill. Maybe he's coming to check up on them to see how we're treating everybody."

The comment caused a check of her priorities. Weston clicked the microphone for a test and her head snapped in his direction. Riley manned a vendor cart selling fruit cups for both human and lemur consumption while Les and Lars stood guard on the far side of the rimming canal. Paisley exhaled.

Kurtis shuffled his feet. "Well, I hope we pass inspection."

"Fear God, not man," she replied, giving him a knowing smile. "Haven't you heard a word Steve's been preaching?"

"Oh, a few of his words have soaked in," he assured her, wiping his cheek.

"I need to get the crowd to shift," she added. "Can you give a whistle?" His piercing blast came too close to her ears, but she covered them to guard from serious damage, and then waved her hands over her head. "Ladies and gentlemen, may I have your attention, please? We're honored to be gaining some late guests who have traveled all the way from Dodge City to attend this afternoon's show. Let's lend them some good old Pawnee Rock politeness and make room. Please let the kids filter down front and sit on the grass, and keep your lawn chairs on the pavement. Thank you very much. We'll start the show once everyone is seated."

A collective mass movement of people played against her orderly mind like an irritating scrape, but she assisted where she could as the local ticket holders obliged the latecomers with little complaint. Younger children made their way to the front lawn and Mimi came out to shower them with attention. She might as well have been wearing a Minnie Mouse costume. For once, Paisley appreciated her theatrical inclination. The chant "I like to move it, move it" went up from their midst, acting like a melodic metronome counting down the delay. When Brace appeared escorting the first wave of immigrants, the seated audience started to applaud in polite welcome.

Kurtis exchanged hand signals with Brace. "Let's get this party started," he sang. The children cheered and Mimi ran for the bridge, touching outstretched palms as she passed.

As seconds ticked by, a feeling of heaviness lifted off Paisley's shoulders and enjoyment began to seep in its place. She stood in one of her favorite spots on earth, ready to perform the two things she loved most, dance and animal handling. Chairs clicked as the bus riders settled, with Brace standing in the middle of the ruckus helping any way he could. She admired him from afar, realizing that her two favorite things had increased to three. When it came their turn to perform, she planned to make that evident. Mr. Granger could pick up on that as well, given his genuine fatherly concern.

Kurtis placed the juvenile lemurs atop a large rock and began to strum his guitar as Mimi moved to the head of the critter dance line. Beyond belief, when she danced forward a step, the lemurs came right with her.

"I like to move it, move it," Kurtis chanted, sounding like an island native. Mimi clapped her hands to the rhythm and soon the entire audience rocked with her. The lemur line circumnavigated the rock mound and split into chaos when Mimi started to sing in a cackling voice. The kids up front lost it with laughter, and the Madagascar-inspired frolic began to crank up momentum.

Paisley glanced at her watch and mentally slid the remaining show schedule back fifteen minutes. Not bad as delays go, plus they had doubled their audience. She glanced over the crowd for Brace and saw him standing beside a man with distinguished gray hair, a cowboy hat in his hand.

"Mr. Granger, I presume," she whispered, striding from behind the crowd to catch Cerise over by the grill. She hoped the gatekeeper was relaying that more hot dogs might need to meet the rotisserie today, as people would be hungry at dinnertime. The built-in intermission would have to slide back as well, but she'd give Amyl a heads-up and ask Les to work in the grill until the dinner rush ended. They could do this, she thought, determined to show Marty how they could step it up with a little help in the right places.

She glanced at Kurtis about the time the lemurs all leaped onto his hulking frame. Mimi exited across the bridge and distributed party hats to the children. She got them to clap and then romped around the compound's moat in a chorus line. Of course they did. Her merriment was full-fledged contagious.

~

The weighted mantle of responsibility rested on his shoulders. Brace brought Sam Gardner's two grandsons inside the aviary atrium. With Cade his only local minion for the performance, Paisley had suggested asking the audience for volunteers. A hunch showed him right where to look. Both boys agreed to eat gelatin like there was no tomorrow, his only prerequisite for the job. Riley crossed the front of the crowd hawking his jiggler wares. The lorikeets skittered off the atrium wall and flew to the back of the cage, startling the newcomers.

Paisley stooped to meet the brothers at eye level. "Remember, the birds won't hurt you."

Cade nodded and clapped his hands together. "We're Ace's men," he replied, shoving four chubby fingers at Brace. "I'll show you guys when to come in. Okay?"

Instead of feeling proud, Brace's confidence wavered, making him check the rings for proper position. Everything seemed in order, but it sure didn't feel that way.

"Great plan," Paisley agreed. "Just be nice to me in the last scene with the marshmallows, right fellas?"

Cade snickered and popped his fist against Brace's knuckles, proving the collusion had already begun.

Paisley turned as she stood ever-so-close and he thought they might have a public face-off, she gazed at him so intensely. "How about we leave it all out there on the floor of the aviary today, my Moorish husband?"

Before he could try to analyze her words, her expression darkened like smoke and she actually winked at him. His fingertips took a stroll across his chin as she stepped away to get in place for her initial dance sequence. Evidently, she hadn't expected an answer.

Cerise began to introduce the altered tale of O-Jell-o and when she spoke the name 'Desdemona' Paisley pushed through the plastic curtain in a fluid sweep, taking his attention with her. She expanded her sequence around the cage, plucking the plastic flower from the perch and tracing her scoop neckline with its petals, then resting it on her cheek like she daydreamed of only her husband, a loyal wife in love. His throat tightened at the connotation. If anything, she was convincing as she left it all on the court today. Well, two could play at that game.

Brace took an exaggerated breath and stepped out on cue, flexing his muscles to assume command of the audience as she gave way. In passing, she twirled and swept by him, her back brushing up against his thin leotard like a suggestion. Unplanned, it brought some heat as the possession arrow switched direction and his gymnastic act began. The worn surface of the rings melded into his grip and he left the earth at the expense of his shoulder muscles, determined to fight gravity using masculine grit. The first few moves became a gyration of exploration, as his momentum carried him deeper into the frenzied routine. When he froze into the iron man pose, the first gasp trembled in from the audience.

He could not see Paisley, but he could somehow sense her on the sidelines, waiting to send the minions out for collaboration. Maybe she could read his body language from there, as he drew the position from vertical to horizontal and the birds broke off the wall to come to him. Amid the flutter, the transfixed audience could barely quell their delight at the scene.

Lowering because his shoulders demanded release, his feet touched the ground and he slowly unfolded his upper body with a hero's glower set in his expression. Once the last bird evacuated the premises, the crowd burst into thunderous applause. He stepped back and motioned for his minions, who tackled his thighs while reporting for duty.

The food cart pushed out behind the huddle and he caught a glimpse of Paisley's face as his eyes traveled up the crimson sleeve of his stage wife. Her neck was stained with a girlish flush which somehow made him soar inside. Transferring his attention to the junior brigade, he stepped toward the food cart and pulled it to center stage. Cerise provided the plot advance as he removed the silver dome and revealed the platter of gelatin squares.

Making a hoggish mockery of Elizabethan manners, the minions slurped with zest and the audience rewarded them with lusty laughs. Before he knew it, Crackers flew toward the group with the traitor's hanky trailing. No amount of jumping by his henchmen could entrap the bird, so he pulled the nectar cup out and Iago responded, along with four other birds suddenly interested in the storyline. His expression marched from gaiety to rage as he choked the lacy cloth while Cerise tightened the plot with narration. Cade pushed the cart backstage before he could remember to snag the rose, leaving him nothing to offer Desdemona in the final scene but a jealous sneer.

Tucking the hanky into his tank top, he snapped off an angry line of round-offs to the back of the enclosure. He opted for one-handed cartwheels upon his return, and dropped into push-up position to regain the birds. They came in a rush of feathers, kneading his back with their claws. More alive than ever, he drew a slow breath and waited for Paisley's return, the crowd's sporadic applause echoing in his ears. A rush of air reported her proximity and the birds startled but didn't flush. Melting down beside him, she feigned an embrace and brushed her arm along his in enticement. Feigning interest, he drew toward her slightly only to snap to his feet repulsed, sending the birds airborne at the marital split-up.

His last combination jerked the rings with authority, as he manifested the Moor's jealousy with a passion. When he felt his shoulders couldn't take another gyration, he lowered himself horizontally toward her reclining figure. As he gained the birds on his back, he held her captive with his gaze.

Off-script, Paisley rose, tucked the tender flower into his shoulder strap, and brushed a kiss against his lips with a faint tremble.

His thoughts rocked with the explosion of touch. All his faculties focused on staying airborne as she gracefully surrendered to her fate, and the minions appeared for the marshmallow pummeling. Cerise brought the tale to its sweetly twisted close and his feet found the aviary floor again for a bow.

Loud applause caused the birds to scatter before he stood fully erect, so he threw a hand of credit skyward and the applause deepened. Paisley emerged from her white-out and smiled, placing a hand in his direction which he readily took. Helping her stand for a bow, he felt the minions' group tackle adhere to his right thigh. Once she stood beside him, he put an arm around her shoulder and drew her in so they were all connected. A lingering peck on the cheek would be all he could afford under so much scrutiny, so he offered it with sweet intent.

Steve had challenged them all to restrain themselves to one kiss per night. This stage kiss had only been a token gesture, but he had every intention to make the real one count. That was leaving it on the court in full, and the court of his choice would be the skyline platform of Pawnee Rock.

~

Maybe she hadn't played fair, Paisley thought, watching the last bus pull out from the base of Pawnee Rock. Adding the scenic stop had been Brace's idea, and Sam Granger had jumped at the opportunity. The Dodge City contingency had taken a flurry of snapshots of the setting sun from the pinnacle before they reloaded in their buses to chase it. The scene fell as a romantic repeat of western heritage preceded by an afternoon of showmanship and innuendo. Kurtis had literally chased Mimi around the mandrill enclosure and Travis melodically pursued Chloe through his harmonica's rendering. Tainted by the lure of love, could the pursuit be all an apparition? If these were rose-colored glasses, she approved of the accommodation as the scenery had grown a little drab before Re-Occupy alighted at the wildlife park.

"Kurtis wants to hang out for the first stars to come out," Brace said from behind her. "You up for that,

Paisley?"

Travis led Chloe back up the sidewalk as Kurtis convinced Mimi to stay. Weston and Riley had stayed behind at the park, stowing the sound equipment for Sunday's encore performance. Les and Lars were nowhere to be found.

"Sure, I guess—for awhile anyway," she replied, her chest tightening a notch as she remembered their first kiss from the top overlook. Chloe and Travis passed as they headed uphill, moving as one body stride for stride. Smiling she recounted all the high school events he'd attended stag-not-drag. God had opened a window of favor, and somehow the residents of bypassed Pawnee Rock were no longer forgotten. A muscular arm slipped around her waist and she yielded to its prompt to start the journey up to the pavilion. Mimi laughed behind her as Kurtis cajoled her into cooperation. The sky gave way from dusky purple to eggplant black, and a pinpoint planet poked out above the horizon.

Travis had already disappeared up the spiral stairway as they stepped in arm-in-arm to the stone-clad fortress. Brace lifted her into his arms before she could react. They ascended the stairs like storybook characters. Her head found his shoulder and a nuzzled kiss worked its way through her hair. As a draft pulled them skyward, she suddenly longed to see an entire splay of stars where the wonderment of God lay hushed.

Brace settled far enough from Travis to give them privacy, but close enough to communicate if needed. Kurtis broke through the upper plane of the stairway to heaven as Mimi giggled from her piggyback position. Brace moved an arm around her shoulders, and she laid her head back in her search for signs of the Almighty in the firmament. Time slipped away, strummed by his fingertips and rendered effervescent by twinkling stars.

"I'm going to miss the show," Travis admitted into the night, followed by a sigh. Kurtis grunted his agreement as Mimi sympathized with a throaty lament.

Brace leaned forward like Roden's Thinker and she rubbed circles on his back. He pulled her to him in slow motion. "What will you miss?' His lips raked her cheek as he spoke.

There could only be one answer and she replied with a tender touch so he wouldn't have to guess. The stars were soon joined by the super nova of his kiss, a light show she'd close her eyes to fully witness.

Chapter 18

Taking up an entire pew in the sanctuary, Re-Occupy had become a cohesive unit at last, Brace reasoned. Steve's sermon on charitable giving that stemmed from a grateful heart came to its conclusion as a pianist began to softly play. Such a miracle to be part of something so ordinary, it seemed extraordinary. It seemed like being home. Paisley shifted as she uncrossed her legs to stand for the benediction.

Lars slid out of the far end of the pew and Steve received him up front with a bowed head and an enfolding arm. Les came down right behind him and nodded when Steve asked him a question. A second arm went around a twin's shoulder and Steve became flanked with Re-Occupy members in adoptive embrace. They trailed back to their seats with hands folded.

Steve stood before the congregation, his head bowed like he had something going on with God. Something like unfinished business, or a matter left to be tended to. When he opened his eyes, they landed right on Brace. Expecting discomfort, he sensed a beckon instead.

Maybe he had already stepped out by the time their shepherd nodded at him. He was a man on the verge.

As he arrived at the front of the platform, Steve retreated up toward the pulpit where the elements of communion could be found on the ordinance table. Brace stood waiting to be claimed like an orphan at a train station. Steve might have known what he was doing, but Brace lacked any clue. Normally standing in front of a crowd empowered him, but that kind of bravado didn't overtake him this morning. Maybe it wasn't supposed to. Empty would come in handy if the Lord could use it.

"God has spoken to my heart through the Holy Spirit this morning," Steve said, his hands pressed together prayerfully, centered on his sternum.

Brace widened his stance to keep from swaying as something moved in his spirit as well. A man's voice murmured "praise the Lord" and several "amens" followed.

"There needs to be a calling out today, a setting aside for the purposes of God. In the Old Testament days, they would term this calling out 'sanctification,' a ceremonial cleansing and dedicated purity purpose. I sense that the Spirit is calling me to anoint Brace Cordan today as a man divinely chosen to follow after God. Are you willing to be obedient, brother?"

Brace started to nod but realized that God required audible confession and public adoration, so maybe he'd appreciate a spoken response now as well. "I humbly obey and consent to the Spirit's leading." The words came from somewhere beyond his thought process. A loath-filled feeling of unworthiness swarmed him immediately and he waivered as though he might run away from God.

Steve descended with an ornate silver flask in his hands, calm and unflappable as their eyes met. "How you feel about yourself has no bearing on this calling. How you think God feels about you has nothing to do with it either. Therefore, may this be of great relief to anyone who thinks himself unworthy to enter into such an intimate relationship with God. By his glory, God hereby separates you, Brace Cordan, from this world and sets you apart for his divine purpose."

The feeling of unworthiness vanished like a mist and Brace stood confident to the task. With methodical precision, hands that once dribbled a basketball down hardwood courts now balanced a vial of blessing over his head in a much more sacred setting, the house of God. A heavy liquid touched his scalp. He closed his eyes to trap the sensation of being anointed.

Somewhere in the background, a woman began to cry, her sobs intoning the solemnity of Steve's ceremony. A bead of liquid ran down Brace's right sideburn and dripped from his chin as Steve continued to pour out the contents of the flask. A sandalwood scent wove the anointment around him and more oil cascaded down his face.

"Sanctified to the glory of God," Steve said at last.

Brace feared opening his eyes to mark the end of the ceremony, as a yearning to stand for God raced through him. Several hushed hallelujahs made their way forward from the congregation. When the Holy Spirit prompted him to open his eyes, his gaze fell onto his Re-Occupy friends. To his absolute amazement, Paisley had been the weeping woman. When their eyes met she looked deeply wounded, like she'd just been stricken by something incurable. A stitch caught under his rib, making it impossible to breathe. Steve gave the benediction and when he lifted his head again, she had vanished.

~

Paisley backed the cart into the dark office already dressed in her costume for the encore performance, trying not to overly converse with God's set apart man while being certain not to touch him. No, she couldn't go there on the Lord's Day.

"Paisley, I'm not going to let Marty blame you for something that was my fault," Brace said, catching several coins as they slid off the food cart. "I forgot to collect the tokens yesterday, not you. Besides, we were all distracted by Sam Gardner's group after the second show. Did Cerise give you his big check?"

She flipped the light switch on and bore a hole in him with her glare. "Yes, she did. Give it a rest, Brace." She tugged at the cart but he wouldn't let it budge, seemingly occupied by something over by Marty's desk. She tracked his gaze and finally saw what he'd been gaping at—an open vault door pointing to a vacated desk. Marty had cleared out after the last show, taking everything of value with him, namely the main computer and the money. She squeezed her eyes closed to choke back the sting of betrayal.

Brace strangled a growl. "He didn't know we'd added the show today."

"So he didn't think we'd find out until Tuesday, good Lord above," she replied, faltering a bit with an uneasy step. "We have to…report this right away. Let me call the sheriff so they can see it before anyone else gets blamed." Her voice came out airy like she'd sprung a leak.

"You mean Re-Occupy?" His brow arched with attitude.

"Or any of yesterday's guests," she added, trying to cover her insinuation. He seemed appeased enough not to ignite the conversation as she pulled out her cell phone and dialed. "Hey, Roy. Paisley St. James here at the wildlife park. Our office got robbed last night. Yeah, can you send someone over? No, we have a show at five, it's better to come on over now. And kill the lights and siren bit, as we want to keep this contained until after the encore show. Thanks. I'll have someone meet you at the front gate." She closed the phone and her eyes began misting as the dread came over her like the plague. "How in the world am I going to keep these animals fed?"

"First, we're going to pray, right here at the crime scene. And then I'm going to head for the front gate and bring the lawman back to you. We have the money on the cart here for the animals. Don't worry, Paisley. We've got a good jump on Marty, and he hasn't had a chance to deposit the money yet, so we can get it back."

"We all worked so hard," she replied, her bottom lip quivering.

Brace took her hands in his and repeated the name of Jesus over and over until he finally launched into fervent prayer for the recovery of the earnings and the future well-being of the wildlife park. After closing the prayer he ran out of the door, leaving it gaping open like a whopper of an unanswered question.

She wandered outside and laid her head against the door jamb, deciding to wait where the scene of trespass wouldn't poke her everywhere she looked. "Why,

God?" She stood off-balance, first with the anointing at church and now the robbery. Only a mourning dove replied, followed by the sound of bleating from the petting zoo. Her world caved in around her, one token's worth of trouble at a time.

She heard the sirens scream as soon as the sheriff's car cleared Pawnee Rock off the highway. The piercing alarm would likely set the animals into panic and the next wave of problems would rear their ugly heads, like uncooperative attitudes in the encore performance. The finicky mandrill flashed into mind and her throat went dry. Mimi would be devastated. Before she could fully collect herself from the last strain of negative thinking, Brace returned with a deputy she didn't recognize.

"Here's Paisley St. James," he said. "She acts as the assistant director of the park, so she had a key to the office. Paisley, this is Deputy Howard."

He took out a notepad from his belt. "Ma'am, tell me how you came about finding the theft, and then I'll look around and call in my report."

"Brace and I brought in the money we collected from the token machines around the park, around one-fifteen," she replied. "When I flipped the lights on, this is what we found. The office had been ransacked, the vault emptied, and the director's computer taken from his desk, right there."

"Did you find the vault open like that?"

Brace crossed the room and stood beside her.

"Yes sir. We haven't touched a thing. I called you on my cell phone."

"Who else works in here that would have a key?"

"I work in here every morning for an hour doing marketing on a secondary laptop, over there," Brace replied. "I never had a key, never needed one as Marty always opened up. He'd be here early counting the gate receipts from the day before."

The deputy looked up from his notes. "Who's this Marty character?"

A weight bottomed out in her stomach, but Paisley knew Brace would hold back and make her put forth the accusation. "Marty Burton, our director. His family owns the park. They're out of Omaha, I think." A searing silence followed. Nothing else was missing except for the lifeblood of the park, money for sustenance, and their high-and-mighty leader.

"Since this cart isn't part of the crime scene, I think you can go ahead and put that change away," the deputy clarified. "I'm going to take a look around the building, both in here and around the perimeter. I'll check anywhere else you might think is important. Does the director live here in Pawnee Rock?"

"No, he takes a seasonal rental in Great Bend for the six months he's down here running the park. I have a cell phone number for him, but no address. He doesn't mix in with the employees too much." Brace hooked an eyebrow at her last comment as she brought her list of contacts up and gave the deputy Marty's cell number. After he strolled around behind the desk looking for evidence, she reached into the cabinet and got the bank bags down.

"Would we be able to block the wildlife park's State Bank account?" Brace asked, causing the deputy to glance up. "Since he took the money Saturday night, maybe he hasn't had a chance to make the deposit…or clean out the account. We've got payroll coming due."

Paisley gasped at the implication of not being able to

pay the staff and the rock in her stomach filled with lead. "We may have the jump on him, as we added the encore show today without his knowledge, so he thinks the park is shut down until Tuesday morning."

The deputy shifted his hat back and gave a strained smile like he didn't get much practice. "We could set up a trap at the bank in the morning," he replied. "Let me get with the sheriff on that, since we're involving a secured area."

Paisley placed a handful of coins into the first bag as the bank's name glared at her from its flank. Brace took a second bag and touched the lose coinage with a look of disdain. Together they got the job done, but she hesitated at what to do with the filled bags. If she kept them until the bank thing blew over, she would have money for animal food later in the week.

Brace approached the deputy. "For the sake of our afternoon show—and the possible bank deal tomorrow, can we try to keep a lid on this theft for now?"

It struck Paisley how protective he was being, keeping the park and its people as top priorities. He became the antithesis of Marty, who had betrayed them all. Her eyes misted again as the personal blow worked its way deeper. They'd worked together for over a decade and now the trust had been violated, a blind backstab if there ever was one.

"That'd be for the best, I believe, given the circumstances," Deputy Howard replied, dropping to his knees behind the desk. Metal scraped the hard tile flooring as the deputy maneuvered, straining at his shoulders. "Does this mean anything significant to you?" His question traced the progression of an ink pen which had a small orange box leveraged on the end.

"Rat poisoning?" Brace asked, frozen stiff with disbelief.

"The animal food station," Paisley squeaked, her throat closing in suffocating reality.

"We have to go check on the animals, sir," Brace added. "They're Paisley's primary responsibility."

She stepped toward the door, unaware if he had released them or not.

"I'll stay here with the money," the deputy replied with a nod. "Come back after you've made your check. I'll call the sheriff in the meantime."

Brace took her arm and ushered her out with an agreeable gesture. Once they'd cleared the doorway, he pulled her close to his side.

"Jesus, help us like never before," he prayed, matching her stride. She sobbed and broke into a run, swamped by the feeling that it could be too late. A high-pitched cry from the guenon cage made her want to retch. Brace pulled her into a detour that took them right up the heart of primate alley. A couple of sharp breaths later, she spotted the mandrill on his circular mission like usual. The baby Schmidt's guenon gave another squeal and pulled its security blanket away from a playful juvenile.

"Enough of that," Brace insisted in a loud voice, pounding the wire. The culprit scampered away and the baby rolled up into the baby blue fleece. "We can't run through the whole park, Paisley. Let's head for the food prep room and try to look for something tainted. You know you're white as a sheet, swirly-girl?"

She turned and hastened away. "Nobody messes with my animals," she replied, unable to gloss over her possessiveness.

"Atta-girl," he replied. "Mama Lion is on the loose now, folks. Stand back and please don't try to pet her rankled mane."

She gave half a laugh, even though it came out more like a hybrid sob, and the exhalation caused her long bangs to fly. Stiff-arming the door open, she pushed up the light switch and began assessing the position of everything on the counter.

Brace followed her in and held his peace.

"Nothing seems to be bothered in here," she relayed.

He touched her shoulder and walked to the refrigerator, pulling the oversized door open. Reaching in, he lifted out a full pitcher of bird nectar, one that she would have delivered to his station in a few hours.

"I didn't make that batch, Brace. We ran completely out after the last performance."

"Are you one hundred percent certain?" he asked, squinting one eye with his interrogation. "I'm not willing to taste-test this, since we're dealing with poison."

She took the lid off and examined the mixture, hoping the color and texture would reassure her. A sticky-sweet smell immediately raised a red flag and she resisted the impulse to pour it down the drain. "Let's go check by the aviary, just to be certain all is well." Opening a lower cabinet, she shoved the pitcher inside for safekeeping. "Lead on, Othello," she insisted, trying not to worry about her lovely feathered friends. They rounded the rhino compound and it sat strangely empty.

"Where's Brutus?" Brace asked, looking all over.

She balled her hands into fists and pressed them onto her temples as if to ward off any further unwanted revelations. Her stomach quivered as she broke into a run toward the aviary. An empty nectar cup caught her eye just outside the plastic curtain and there, beside the perch, lay a little yellow and red lifeless lump. "Please no. Not Crackers…" The air leaked completely out of her lungs. She dropped to her knees outside the front wall, clutching the wire mesh for stability as her entire world turned upside down in a color-filled splat.

Chapter 19

I need to tell you something before we go back to the deputy," Brace said. He pulled Paisley to her feet and locked her in a no-nonsense gaze. When she trembled in his grip, regret rippled through his veins. "Come on, let's walk through the park and check the other animal stations. We'll take the kangaroo court past the petting zoo and end up at the lemurs."

"I can't take any more bad news, Brace," she replied, ashen and reflexive while withdrawing from him.

He couldn't blame her if things might not be the same between them once he got this off his chest. He'd spent four years digging this pit and now it was his to claim. "Okay, let's just walk for now." Delay had been his tactic all along hadn't it? First delay by avoidance. Then delay by diversion with Re-Occupy. It all added up to lack of productivity, a personal failure he'd been remiss in addressing. That he was gainfully employed now might not serve to knock any tarnish off his record. He was in too deep, and now he had the nerve to drag Paisley in with him. The albino alligator hissed and thrashed as they walked by.

"I feared the sirens would put the animals on edge and it looks like I was right," she lamented, turning toward Lemur Island.

"Let's go sit in with the lemurs and get them to calm down," he said, thinking that they might lend a comical diversion to his pending admission. The boulders anchoring the exhibit weren't the only hard thing in the picture. By the time his foot hit the bridge, he remembered to pray and release the issue to God. It was all he could do at this point. He waited for her to perch on a relatively flat rock and he sat opposite her so they could regard one another. No more dodging, the time had come for a direct encounter with the truth.

"Paisley, I'm not a free man—not as free as you think I am," he began. Already he needed to swallow and regroup his courage. She looked fearful, too wounded to withstand his verbal admission, but he had seen her inner strength before and had to count on it. "I haven't honored God with my finances. As part of my financial aid package at the university, I accepted student loans every year. Focused on my double major, I didn't watch the accrual rate as I worked toward graduation. In the end, I owed in the vicinity of thirty thousand dollars."

Her mouth dropped open but no words of judgment came, simply astonishment.

"You see why I need to tell you that right now," he continued. He wanted to reach out for her hand, but didn't deserve the redemption of it. He felt leprous like an outcast, which is probably why he'd affiliated with Re-Occupy to start with, not because he was anti-establishment. "The sheriff will look for probable cause, and when they find out I have outstanding debt…"

"Brace, you didn't do it," she replied, pulling the juvenile lemur off her shoulder. Its cousin came over and sat in her lap. "You were in the crow's nest with Weston and Riley last night and in church being anointed for special purpose this morning. Regardless of that, you've been doing everything in your power to make this place better, student debt or no student debt."

"And I've started payments, Paisley. I paid in double for my first payment which Dad turned in a month early. I feel good about all of that, but what I feel the worst about is…not telling you right up front. Believe me, I tried to keep my distance until I began the debt payment. I tried not to get you tangled up in my problems."

"How did that go?" She caught two lemurs in a hug. A large female came and encircled her neck like a scarf.

He would have laughed if he hadn't been so disappointed with himself. A tug down below revealed he was having his shoes untied. "Horrible. From the first day you rescued me from the outhouse, I was hooked like a sap." It occurred to him that she might take offense at that so he ran his fingers over her arm. She patted the back of his hand. The alpha male came up beside him and patted his other hand in mocking empathy.

"You need to know about ROZ," she replied, picking up a baby lemur. She caressed its forehead which further accentuated its big eyes.

Even the animals were moping for him. "So, is that one Roz?" he asked, trying to gain some understanding.

"No, silly. The governor's ROZ. It stands for Rural Opportunity Zone initiative. Barton County is one of seventy-three counties in the state of Kansas looking for new residents. Mom served on the promotion committee because our county had to opt in—which it did last year. Anyone moving here from out-of-state is eligible for a state income tax exemption for five years. Any of you Re-Occupy members could settle down here and claim it."

The unease hoisted beneath his sternum slipped a bit, as she shined some light down his dark tunnel instead of judging him. "And I could use that tax savings…to accelerate payments on my student loan debt," he added, his gaze tripping beyond the island to see a greater horizon.

"Brace, ROZ has a student loan forgiveness clause as well," she said, taking his hand with a gentle squeeze. "There's a maximum amount, I think around fifteen thousand, for a college graduate who moves into a ROZ county and uses his major in a profession."

Something near the bottom of his lungs trembled, sending a quake through the rest of him. Half of his student loan could be obliterated just by living in Pawnee Rock. He couldn't overcome the sensation that the way was somehow being paved for him to come here, a work of providence filtered through the capital in Topeka and legislated like forgiveness of an ill-begotten loan."What would I have to do?" he asked, too incredulous to think rationally.

"Establish permanent residence and file the ROZ paperwork. Eventually you might have to show some proof of residency, like a power bill or something."

"Can I do that from the crow's nest? I could, right?"

"No, Leta's been down that road before with the post office. They wouldn't give her last missionaries their own mailing address up there." She sighed and pulled another lemur off her torso, standing to leave. "There is a way around it, though."

"What's that, I'll do it tomorrow," he pledged, standing with her. Lemurs filled the spots they had vacated on the rock, moving like fur balls in his peripheral vision. Paisley had his full attention as they conspired to get him ROZ-certified and shed of half his debt.

"You can have my upstairs apartment with its separate utility bill and established address." She shrugged her shoulders. "You need it and I don't…so we'll swap."

Now he became dumbfounded at the turn of events, as not only was she not judging him, she offered the only working solution at her own expense. He became as undone as his shoelace. "Paisley…how could I?" Having debated the finer points of a hundred civic issues, his mind somehow could not grasp a single leverage point to counter her reasoning. This was not logic—it ran insanely deeper. "I'm not worth all the trouble."

"Remember what Steve said? It doesn't matter what you think about your own worthiness, you're here to do a work of God, anointed for it, truth be told. Had you ever thought that you might have been brought here at just the right time—for us?" She gestured out into the park as she started out over the bridge.

His breathing only came in half-exhalations as he followed her, his mind swimming in consideration. Everything from his sickness onward had been building up to the calamity they faced at the wildlife park, not his own personal tragedy. All he had to do was live here permanently and half his debt would melt away. But what about the wildlife park? It still teetered on the brink. Maybe one man could make a difference, one airborne man with some determination and a flashy public relations degree.

~

Paisley had lost track at Cerise's gate count of four hundred, as the pressing crowd teemed toward Lemur Island. The church had loaned its folding chairs for patrons who arrived without a seat, and Steve worked with the twins to get several rows lined up in an arc around the moat. Brace floated through the arrivals, shaking hands and expressing his personal thanks for their participation. From time-to-time, his laugh echoed across the lawn which made the situation bearable for her. Having packed out the park took the edge off her financial worries. The rest she'd already given to the Lord. Anger at Marty led the pack, but there were other insecurities bundled in there, too.

Mimi snuck up behind her. "Remember what we vowed in the staff huddle, right?"

She stiffened her spine and pulled at the neckline of Desdemona's endowment, nodding at the shorter player who had proven to be a powerhouse in her own right. "Give our best, as unto the Lord," she replied, releasing an authentic smile.

"One more time for all the old times," Mimi sang, a happy lilt in her voice. "I see lots of romantic couples in the crowd, so I might play up to that, if you think it's appropriate." Her voice rose, coming more like a question.

Paisley touched her shoulder to extend permission. "Maybe the crazy performance with the mandrill would be better suited," she suggested, giving Mimi something to think about. When the singer gave a little twist, her netting-fluffed skirt dipped. Paisley knew something special was brewing within the teapot. Mimi flashed a peace sign with her fingers, which she immediately confused for an indication of the second act.

No matter, they needed all the appeal they could muster. It started with the Re-Occupy addition of slightest stature. She would raise the bar for everyone. Desdemona would have to reciprocate or smother trying. Well, she could at least match Mimi's enthusiasm.

The Madagascar frolic ran its course with more mayhem than usual as the baby lemurs attached themselves to Kurtis and Mimi with regularity like stick-on fixtures. Les had the idea to reward twenty lucky crowd members with winning tokens and a trip inside the island complete with dried cranberry treats. Cameras clicked non-stop as the lemurs launched their attack on the unsuspecting winners, making for an out-of-control, up-close wildlife encounter that turned out to be a real crowd pleaser.

Paisley glanced at her watch for the time delay but didn't think it mattered given the entire scheme of things. The last show claimed its own freedom, so she took some comfort from that realization. Riley had retreated with the empty food cart which was Cerise's cue to invite their guests to the next venue—the aviary.

Her thoughts dashed to the dead bird resting in a cup box under the foyer shelf. As much as it hurt to think of Crackers being gone, there were larger hurts still set to take wing. She entered the aviary intent on bringing another bird into training at the last minute. One of the larger birds swooped toward her and she rewarded it with a cranberry torn in half. She stroked the bird and then affixed the hanky on its leg, allowing it several moments to get adjusted.

Feeding the second half of the reward, she pushed the bird into flight and watched it loop around the perimeter. Once it returned, she pulled off the talisman of betrayal and stowed it near the food cart. Scanning the tray, she lifted the dome to find fresh squares of jewel-colored gelatin in place for the scene. Amyl had a big thank-you coming after they survived this onslaught. She spotted the rose a second before Brace entered the foyer.

He touched the small of her back. "Are we good to go here?"

She nodded with a smile. "The hanky will fly with one of the big birds. I just took him on a test flight and it looked pretty solid."

His eyes sparkled in admiration. "You're the best—you know that?" His voice sounded husky with personal attention. Four little minions ran inside.

The private moment shattered, but she thought she might know how to recapture it, thanks to Mimi. "Go check your apparatus while the crowd shifts over. Everything will take a little longer to set up today, but praise God for the logistics of a record-breaking crowd."

He shouldered through the plastic curtain and several birds fluttered from the cage wall. Children gathered outside the aviary and Brace rewarded their attention with a short warm-up routine on the rings. He clapped his hands at them and a puff of chalk went airborne.

After a run-through with the minions at the food cart, her gaze landed on the rose. Something in that exchange could be embellished, she thought. Maybe something a loving, unsuspecting wife might do. Heat flushed her neck as she remembered his command for mulberry, which assured him of an intimate brush. This time she'd knock him off his rings. Wasn't that what an encore was for?

The plan fell into place with proper emotion and sequencing. When Cerise made her introduction, Paisley took the aviary floor with a flourish that would make every eye turn her way. The oh-so feminine costume pulled below the balls of her shoulders and she let it stay. The dance ended with open exuberance and she played a hand across Brace's chest as she exited.

He took to the rings and gave a truly inspirational performance. When he leveled to horizontal from the iron cross, the big bird came first, leading the rest. Admiration held at a hushed level until he dropped to the ground, where it exploded from the crowd and sent the birds back to the wire.

She pushed the food cart out behind the antsy minions, making sure Brace saw her longing expression. The hanky launched without a hiccup and the minions set free with their bird-chasing scamper. Brace countered in reactive gymnastics for his jealousy scene, setting the stage for her reappearance.

Her second dance centered fully on him, every flounce and unrequited reach of her arms. She went to the floor under the rings and he went aerial. At last he tipped horizontal and the birds flew to them both, feeling like a blessing from heaven above.

Brace pulled the rose loose with his mouth and she

lifted to meet him. With a graceful touch of her hand, she slid the flower from its setting and closed the distance separating them. The longing now at full crest, she brought her lips up to his.

"I love you, Ace," she whispered, ending with a fully-executed kiss. He trembled at her touch which she found most pleasant as Desdemona relinquished to her unfortunate end. The marshmallows came in a flurry, and the audience transitioned from one emotion to the next with unfettered laughter. They couldn't hear her laughing, too, but she felt freed from worry—even under an avalanche of puffed confection.

Cerise finished out the epilogue, twisting comedy from tragedy. She couldn't help but feel her day had taken the same turn. With the minions already bowing incessantly, Brace pulled her to her feet and lifted her like she'd become the aerialist. And in his arms, she did fly. When her feet touched the ground, he tugged her into a bear hug and the audience voiced their approval.

"You're the only one for me, swirly-girl," he whispered in her ear.

Her hands found the hills of his shoulders and took hold, savoring the landscape of the moment. She'd gone from blatantly robbed to fully bestowed, all in one afternoon. With God, all things were indeed possible. No wonder the audience had to clap.

Chapter 20

L ess off the top, but scrape the sides down like a regular cut." Brace chopped at the plastic cape as Leta revved up the clippers to start his shearing. When Paisley brought a tray of cinnamon rolls over, he helped himself to a rather large specimen. A glass of milk appeared next over the bar while his stylist paused long enough for him to reach it.

"So you're good with this switch, Leta?" Paisley asked, pointing first to her former upstairs apartment and then the crow's nest. Without glancing away from her task, the landlady nodded her approval, bending Brace's head forward to carve out a stopping point in back.

A bundle of wavy black hair cascaded to the floor signaling change. In a handful of minutes, Brace felt lighter and somewhat relieved, like the style session came way past due. "We have to be in Great Bend by nine, so how are we doing?" he asked, unable to see the clock.

Paisley flashed him a thumbs-up and took a bite out of her roll. Weston and Riley banged through the back door as if following the baking aroma to the kitchen. They walked right in and helped themselves, a reflection of their landlady's open-door generosity.

Brace smiled and tried to look up, but Leta corrected his head position and more hair fell across his right ear.

"Morning fellas," Paisley said. "We have to go into Great Bend first thing here, so we'll do the move sometime around lunch. Okay?"

"Fine with me," Weston replied, chomping into the pastry treat. Riley merely lifted his newly poured glass of milk which Weston eyed with covetous regard.

"We're bringing food back for the animals, so don't bother with feeding up while we're gone," Brace added. "Remember, we've got to dispose of that poison mixture, so just stay out of the food prep room." When Paisley looked like she'd been hurt physically, he gave her a wink that became muted under a cascade of clipped locks.

She stepped over and wiped his brow clear, puffing cinnamon breath onto his face. "This is turning out to be quite the sheep shearing." Riley laughed and reached for a second roll.

"We're meeting Les and Lars at ten o'clock for trash cleanup around the grounds," Weston said. "Steve arranged for a Cub Scout troop to come give us a hand when he heard about the big crowd last night. Cerise claimed the gate total came to four seventy-five."

Brace ducked under Leta's hand and attempted the mental math for his escalator pay—if they could afford to make payroll at all. He thought about the receipts Paisley had waiting to deposit and he wondered how to proceed. They couldn't deposit in the park's regular account until the sheriff's shakedown. "You know, it's too bad the community couldn't own the park."

Leta's hands froze over top of his head and the clippers soon came clattering down on the table. "Brace Cordan, you're a genius," she quipped, regaining the scissors to snap them in thin air. Tufts of hair departed from the crown of his head, much to his immediate alarm.

"Leave me some waves to play with," Paisley replied, shooting him a redeeming look. "Now let's pursue this community-owned idea. How could we go about that? I think we'd have some ready-to-invest local supporters."

He licked the sugar off his lips and gave it some thought. "Say we catch Marty red-handed trying to close the park's State Bank account, or make the deposit in his new account at Capitol Merger," he began, laying some card options on the table. "We could have a plea-bargain deal ready for the Burton family's consideration. Reduce the charges against Marty for an agreement to allow Pawnee Rock to buy out their interest in Tanah Keeta. We could offer public shares, and then anyone could buy stock in the company."

"But first we'd have to come up with the buy-out money, right?" Paisley asked, rubbing the rim of her glass.

Leta worked up toward his bangs and went light on the clipping, allowing a wave of hair to cascade down his forehead. With a last snip, she discarded the scissors and began to hum as she combed through Brace's hair one last time. The plastic cape came off with a crackle.

He stood up to shake off the hair stubble around his collar. "And money is what we don't have." He folded his arms around his volunteer stylist as payment. Her eyes twinkled as the hummed melody continued. He attacked the cinnamon roll platter and motioned at the chair with his latest conquest. Weston accepted the invitation and sat, shaking his straight sandy hair until it obscured his eyes. Leta stepped out to the sunroom and shook the cape out the backdoor, seeming ever so happy to have another customer.

"Somebody's hiding something," Paisley hinted in a soft sing-song voice.

The elderly woman returned and snapped the cape into place, pausing to take his order.

"A little off everywhere," Weston replied. "Make me pretty, so I can get a girl like Brace did." He kicked at his shoe.

"Well, Effie's daughters have just come back from their trip to Spain for college credit," Leta shared. "Maybe they could help with the cleanup around the park today. You know what they say—the more, the merrier."

Brace started to laugh and glazed sugar went everywhere.

"You're incorrigible, Leta," Paisley replied, dodging his pinch.

"You should make that call to Effie," Brace added with a knowing look.

Leta pointed the clippers and revved them up like a woman with a plan. "Okay, Riley, you're next. You have such lovely eyebrows—but no one can see them."

"I'm going to pack," Paisley added, resting her glass on the bar. "If you guys can bring the cots down to the driveway, I can take them back while we're in town."

"You're going to put my roomies on the floor?"

Brace replied, his newly shorn locks now freeing his expressiveness. He waggled his eyebrows to prove it.

She smirked in return. "It's a two-bedroom apartment, Brace, with real beds and everything."

His cheeks reddened at the disclosure that he was set to move up in the world with his new permanent address—all coming at her expense.

"Trades are seldom fifty-fifty." She turned and headed up the stairwell.

Brace gave her claim some thought. He'd have to try real hard to find a way to level out the uneven balance, one that wouldn't cheat her end of the deal. Sure, he needed her real address, but he didn't need her amenities, as though they were moveable—or could be.

~

At two minutes after nine, Deputy Howard walked into the president's office at State Bank where they were sequestered. Paisley drew a deep breath, keeping her mind calm and open to input. She had to remain rational for the sake of the park. Brace stood silently at her side.

"Mr. Burton already packed up his apartment," the deputy disclosed, tucking his thumbs in his utility belt. "It's anyone's guess whether he'll come here next, or whether he's already hit the road—which would make our job a little tougher."

"We've been pulling in some big gates with this Shakespeare Festival," Brace replied. "My bet is that he's coming to cash those in and then close out the account. He wouldn't want to take a loss on the personal checks people used for admittance, as he gives a discount for cash and checks so he can have the money at his disposal quicker."

"Good point, Brace," Paisley added. "We've done that for years, so our repeat customers typically take advantage of it."

"In the future, we should consider family membership discounts," Brace said.

The deputy tossed a searching look between the two of them. "I take it you two expect to survive this management coup." An angular smile marked his stoic face.

Brace shuffled his feet and glanced at her.

"Yes, sir. I'll step up, as necessary, and take us forward," she replied.

"But she'll have the support of the rest of us," Brace added, touching her elbow.

A surge of assurance seeped through her as the bank president came into the room. "We have the wildlife park's balance safely secured in the new account under your signature for now, Miss St. James. After we see how this shakes out, we'll offer you something more permanent." He shook her hand and then gave it a pat, nodding to Brace.

"And the money Marty is trying to deposit?" she asked.

He gave her a slow wink and motioned toward the deputy. "Today's transaction will go into the new account for holding until we see what the legal ramifications are. Since you're already a signatory for the existing account, I have no qualms whatsoever."

"Then I wish my qualms could be alleviated that easily." Paisley kneaded her hands together. That gave him an opportunity to laugh. She'd never heard a banker laugh before. It had quite a medicinal effect.

"My dear, you have more local support than you

could ever imagine. That tenacious wildlife park has been our little regional darling for a long time. I think my Mildred plans to come out in a couple of weeks, as a matter of fact."

"Yes, sir. Her Federated Women's Club has their annual tea with us in August. We add a few frills to our presentation for that group, which makes it extra fun for us."

"And hence, extra work—but you're a real saint for not admitting it. So my advice is to let the community go to bat for you today. I have your back here at State Bank, and the good deputy here will set the trap. We simply need you to make sure we have the right man. Is that a deal?"

"Well, when you put it like that," she replied with a fidget.

He pumped her hand one last time and released it, returning to his desk. The radio on Deputy Howard's shoulder reported a single click and he tapped at it in response. She stiffened her back and found Brace's hands balanced on her shoulders. She could feel the encounter coming. The confrontational aspect sickened her stomach, but she wouldn't let Marty get away with this—for the park's sake.

Seconds scraped off the clock and the teller's signal came over the president's phone as planned. He exited around the desk and tucked his tie back into his jacket. She shrunk back as he went by, only to find Brace's hand on the small of her back. Trying to overhear the conversation out in the lobby, her own pulse deafened her ability. The deputy hugged the door frame, maintaining his stealth position as long as possible.

Now she could hear Marty's stern objection to the

park's balance being zeroed out. The president attempted to placate him with a calm demeanor, but Marty escalated the threat to demand all the money.

The deputy held up one hand and methodically dropped one finger at a time until nothing but a fist was left. He paused in the doorway long enough to insure the teller had cashed out the latest deposit and then he walked out to represent the strong arm of the law.

Paisley moved toward the door trying to catch a glimpse of the encounter. To her amazement, a well-dressed woman stood beside Marty while trouble broke loose. She looked indignant for the delay.

Deputy Howard took the teller's envelope from Marty and forced his hands behind his back. Brace gave her a tap and they stepped out together to make the identification.

"Miss St. James, is this the man who had access to the vault?" the deputy asked.

"Yes, that's the park director, Marty Burton. He took our money, packed up his computer, stole our rhino, poisoned the lorikeets, and left us for helpless losers," she replied, venom spicing every word.

"Why, you little imp," Marty replied. The deputy jerked him back while the woman took a step away to dissociate with the perpetrator, a move that came a little too late.

"We were supposed to elope today," she said, guarding the designer handbag she carried.

"Hush up, Verna," Marty demanded, his neck turning scarlet red. "My family owns this park, so I have every right to take the money."

"We have sworn affidavits from your family members that you are supposed to be operating as usual until the park shuts down for the season on October first," the deputy replied.

Marty shut his gaping jowls in astonishment. The deputy began reciting his Miranda rights as Brace gave her a clandestine look. Maybe "The Tempest" concluded with something more tangible than dreamlike magic this time with an outcome that gave the distinct appearance of justice.

"Would you like to tell us about your unauthorized deposits at Capitol Merger Bank where all our clouded leopard money went?" Paisley posed. She had a new affection for disclosure, as it seemed to point to the truth of the matter.

"Talk to my lawyer," Marty grumbled, hanging his head.

"Ma'am, you can walk along with us all cooperative-like," the deputy suggested, "or I can find a new bracelet for you, too. Until we find out whether you've been an accessory to this crime, we need to have you with us."

Verna shifted in her high heels. "Oh, all right," she replied, her glossy coral lipstick accentuating her surrender. "Some wedding day...I want my one phone call."

"I bet you do," the deputy replied. He nodded to the bank president who followed along behind. Brace pulled her into a hug and spoke a comment not fit to share.

"Miss St. James?" The teller beckoned to her, waving the deposit envelope. "Should I?"

"Goodness, yes," she said, approaching the counter. "Into the park's new account, please. I've got payroll to make by the end of the week." The simple statement sounded promising, like business would go on despite criminal intent at the upper level. Like a clouded leopard, she'd landed back on her feet.

~

The bonfire took the last ache of the day from his shoulders, as Brace mentally retraced his steps from Great Bend to the new upstairs apartment. Mesmerized by the flames, he let the fire's dance shave the sharp edges off all the day's unanswered questions.

"Thank you for the offer to pay everyone," Travis said, pulling Chloe tighter.

"You're welcome—and beyond," Paisley replied. "Guys, about the festival this year."

"We kept the party moving," teased Mimi, scrunching into Kurtis.

"And don't forget Chromeo, plus O-Jell-o and his gelatin-slurping minions," Edgar added.

"How could we forget?" Cerise replied with a furtive look his way.

"We'll be going back to school in a couple of weeks," Weston admitted.

"But we'll never forget this summer," Riley added.

"We should do a farewell party. You know, an end-of-summer blow-out," Kurtis said.

Now that was an idea Brace could warm up to. He sat forward to address the troupe. "How about after the Federated Women's tea party on the tenth? We could let the decorations double for a staff party and kick back together one last time."

"You know, we always try to open the park to the public one evening before school starts," Paisley replied. "We could invite them out at twilight and let them see the eye-shine of the animals. I think that would be memorable.”

"Sounds like a flashlight party. Let's do it. Guys, what do you say?" Brace asked. Affirmatives rang in, and he searched the fire's core to find a way to offset Paisley's greater sacrifice. He simply had to.

Chapter 21

Once Marty had been held without bail, Paisley received the Burton family's permission to resume operation until the seasonal closing date. At that juncture, she had requested their openness to entertain an offer for possible transfer of ownership, delicately lacing her wording to hint at the plea bargain potential for their ill-fated son. She had a feeling that they would be receptive, given the dire situation. She straightened a gold-leaf doily on the white tablecloth and assessed the pavilion. It certainly looked like a party or two lurked on the horizon. A Colobus monkey squawked nearby, making her eye the empty rhino pen.

Were she truthful with herself, removal of the larger animal came as a relief. Now they wouldn't have to feed such a bulky program animal all winter, which left more funding for the small fries. Plus, they'd reclaimed the selling price for Brutus, putting almost ten thousand dollars in the park's new account. A flash of blue fleece caught her eye as the baby Schmidt's guenon scampered from one end of the cage to the other. She laughed and stepped toward the grill to check on Amyl and the special fare for the Federated Women's tea party.

Brace had been insightful to suggest loaning out the fertile clouded leopard pair to the Omaha zoo, again lightening the load. Unwilling to sell, she liked this loan agreement as it gave her some leverage for payback. For now, she'd allow for the transfer of possession and decide in the spring what would benefit them the most. Strategizing came with a kick of power, which she enjoyed more than she would admit. God had been preparing her for leadership all these years and here she was, finally carrying it out. Metal clinked against metal as she rounded the grill's counter toward the ordering window.

"How's it coming, Amyl?" she called, seeing his back as he lowered a tray on the food cart's bottom rack.

"They are going to love my popovers this time, Paisley," he replied. "It's ready to go."

"Perfect, Amyl. You're doing a remarkable job this summer. I wanted you to know."

"Thanks. I so appreciate the extra helping hands from the Re-Occupy guys."

"Well, make sure to let them know at the staff party afterward," she replied. "I'm all done out here. I'll go wait by the front gate for the ladies of Great Bend." She bowed and left the pavilion, inspecting the animal cages as she came up. Everything looked ready. Seeing the aviary empty, she wondered where Brace had been keeping himself lately. Mystery floated in the air. She untangled a wayward plastic bag from a landscape hedge and made tracks for the entrance.

Cerise saluted her as she stepped into view and a

commotion in the parking lot snagged her attention. Several guys were heaving a large structure from the back of a truck. As they walked closer, she recognized Les and Lars on the front end of a wooden arch. The rest of the truss came into view and Kurtis huffed to keep up pace with the others.

"So, what do you have here, fellas?" she quipped, trying to remember if they'd discussed this addition for the party.

"Special delivery," Brace replied from the far side.

A curious look came over Kurtis' face. "Goes with your theme of 'Summer Love' doesn't it?"

"Why, yes it does—which makes you Cupid's helpers—or what?" she teased, standing aside to allow them entrance. She glanced at Cerise who looked away, feigning any knowledge of the arrival. It quickly occurred that she was the odd man out. Chloe stepped up from the parking lot joined by Effie's daughters who had volunteered to serve. They all had wispy dresses on, making her regret her animal handler uniform instantly. Maybe she'd run back to the crow's nest between parties and girl-up her appearance a bit, if time allowed. A caravan of luxury sedans pulled in the parking lot next, announcing the arrival of the Federated Women's Club.

"And so yet another program begins at the gathering place," she quipped.

~

Brace tied off the last can liner and pulled it loose, setting it on the wheeled cart Amyl used to make the trash run. From the look of things, the tea-and-crumpet gang had really lived it up. With Paisley's tour ending at the petting zoo, he gave them half an hour tops to be done and out of the facility. He glanced at his watch and gave Travis less time than that to appear. This would be a monumental day for him, but Brace would have to keep that in his chest pocket for now. The twins came back from Lemur Island in animated conversation with Effie's daughters. A Spanish exclamation reverberated above the group, chased by mocking laughter.

"Summer Love," he recited, glancing around the park. Time sure had done a number on him this summer, including a trip down lover's lane. He eyed the arch and went over to straighten the corded lights, placing the plug-in near the outlet. Having decided that "Tunnel of Love" was too revealing, he'd chosen to name the structure "Tunnel of Truth" instead. The truth would turn to love when it became appropriate, which would be remarkably soon.

He had a nugget of truth to divulge, as well—one that floated down to him which didn't require much panning from the sluice. How they would receive it was another matter. His stomach turned and he reconsidered the economics of it as a business venture. Much more than that, it would place them at a turning point that would require both holding on and letting go. The source of the offer deserved a response, and he'd vowed to get it tonight or decline in default.

"Lord, help me with this one. It's beyond me, but not too big for you," he admitted in prayer, mumbling around the pavilion. The Spanish speakers came in and the twins settled onto a far table, still showering the women with rapt attention. Edgar brought Cerise up from the front gate, and Amyl made his trademark trip to the dumpster without much ado. Weston stepped into the pavilion and gave in to his techie side, stooping to plug in the light cord. He waved a greeting and turned to find Riley helping Amyl at the dumpster. That had been the summer in a nutshell, help whenever it was needed and a team approach to every task.

Brace had always dreamed of being a part of something like this, team-tackled and cohesive. Structured but still leaving room to move. Responsible yet creative. All things he could lose himself in. But Re-Occupy hadn't been like this at all. In fact, it had been almost the opposite. Only God could have redirected him so completely, turning him one hundred-eighty degrees. Making him stay and embrace instead of traipsing around the countryside. There was something redemptive about that, about this whole place. Maybe when it came his turn to stand inside the "Tunnel of Truth," he could be candid about some of this revelation. He could be real.

"Hey, man," Kurtis said, stepping onto the pavilion floor with Mimi at his side. "Is Paisley coming soon?" Mimi wrinkled her nose at him like some kid sister.

"Dude, I hope so, as the breeze is blowing over a lonely man right now," he replied, pressing a hand against his chest. The gentle giant slapped a sympathetic hand across his shoulder and headed down to the far table to harass the twins. Cerise came in giggling at Edgar's last joke, looking chummy by his side.

"Welcome to what's left of Summer Love," he teased, sipping from an imaginary cup. Cerise looked at Edgar and blushed, then managed to giggle again. Those two would need some time to gel, he thought, sensing some immaturity. Edgar had mentioned plans for community college in the fall, which would only serve him well. They drifted down the pavilion as Amyl came back and began washing the cart down.

Brace walked around the building to help, and Riley turned the faucet on to get the job done. The physical exertion came like a balm, as his stomach seemed unsettled about the pending decision. He couldn't let that ruin his end-of-summer party with his peers, though. Amyl signaled him away, and Riley gave the cart a final blast. More than ready for the party to begin, he turned to find Travis coming up the walkway swinging hands with Chloe. Now the gears were in motion.

He took an inventory and everyone was accounted for except Paisley. They could chat it up casually for awhile and give her a few minutes to transition from work to play. After all, the park was officially closed the next two hours until the gates opened to the entire community at dusk. Wiping his hands at the napkin dispenser on the condiment shelf, he migrated down to the action zone and fell into conversation to bide his time.

Soon a nudge teased him from behind and he turned to see someone standing in a blue sheer dress, its hem flattered by the breeze. Paisley's hair looped up on top of her head damsel-style, making her eyes sizzle above porcelain cheekbones. He regarded her like he'd never quite seen her before and somehow he couldn't breathe. Kurtis busted him with a flattened palm to bring him back to consciousness. He swallowed trying to regain his composure. Travis hinted something about the tunnel and Mimi winked a cue to liven him up. He stood and touched Paisley's elbow in passing, heading for the arch. Tongue-tied and awkward, he turned and faced his friends.

Mimi laced her arms around Kurtis. "Aw look. Ace finally let the cat get his tongue." The guys laughed like that had never happened before.

He swiped his nose and let the smirk turn into a smile as he opened himself up to the truth. Paisley sat on the edge of the picnic table, her attention focused on the speaker. "Is there any other place on earth like this?" he began, sincerity weaving his words together. He heard "amen" above the other murmurs as Amyl and Riley joined the gang and settled in.

"Some of the guys thought it would be nice to have this handsome focal point for our party. Let's give them a hand for building a masterpiece that we can use for seasons to come." A spattering of applause followed, along with a few jeers. "I've dubbed this thing the 'Tunnel of Truth,' thinking it might be meaningful to us if we shared from the heart what this summer has meant to each of us. Anybody want to go first?"

"Allow me," Weston insisted, stepping form the group. Some heckling calls followed him up, so he waited them out with a crooked smile. "I'm going to look back on this summer with memories of the nicest community I've ever had the good fortune to be a part of. That started the night we came into town."

"Midnight—by truck," Kurtis called out with a laugh.

"What an entrance, huh? But we were taken right in. Miss Leta has been awfully sweet, providing for us every way she knew how, cinnamon rolls in the morning, haircuts, and rides into church. The church, it's congregation, Steve and his wisdom from God, his words aptly spoken, all these are part of my memory for the summer. Let me also include the animals here in the park, these phenomenal animals that keep us so mindful of God and his creativity. I've gone doggone soft on these animals, especially that baby monkey running around with the blue blanket."

"Hands off my baby guenon," Paisley replied, crossing her arms possessively.

Brace gave her a wink and felt her presence like a tidal wave. Weston put a hand to his heart and bowed, ending his time of sharing.

Without having to be called out, Lars stepped up next. "This has become a place of sheer humility for me," he admitted, his voice wavering. Several female voices coaxed him onward and he collected himself. "Playing basketball beside Steve Ryland made me feel like a dwarf novice, even though I've been playing the game all my life. That was truly iron-sharpening-iron for me, as his spiritual leadership exceeded his ball handling, and made me wake up to a few areas of omission in my life. You guys let me be myself, body humor and all…"

"Oh, Chromeo," Kurtis teased, morphing into a heckler.

"What an alter-ego, right? But truly, I'm stoked about what I've discovered in the shadow of Pawnee Rock this summer and thrilled to be taking back four new friends to campus this fall. That said, you guys are the best." He left the tunnel and Mimi popped up.

Brace had a feeling it had turned time for soppy cute, but he wouldn't censor Mimi, no matter what.

"Fellas, you know all about Mimi, right?" she began, a tease in her voice.

When she turned toward Brace, he saw the shimmer of tears welling up in her eyes. Okay, that was unexpected.

"Or maybe you don't, but since I'm standing in the 'Tunnel of Truth'—well, here it is. I am happy for the first time in my life, truly happy. Every part of this place makes me feel secure, safe, and free to be me. It brings a song to my lips and a swagger to my hips." Her little hip nudge gave Kurtis the opportunity to express his pleasure cowboy style—loud and wild.

"I need to thank Brace for bringing me back here or I would have never known what it could feel like to be this alive," she added, the tears arriving full force now.

His throat closed with her sincerity, so he swallowed to keep it open.

"You see, I met Kurtis the night Brace came back to rescue us in Dodge City. How do you say thanks for something that changes your whole life like that? Want the moon, Ace? I got nothing but empty hands and open-hearted thanks." She blew him a kiss and headed back to the huddle where Paisley waited for her with open arms.

Edgar stepped up like Willy Wonka, doing a forward roll from a rehearsed stumble and popping up to a trickle of applause. "I consider this summer the debut of my comedic career. Thank you, Brace and Paisley, for tugging us out of our comfort zones and presenting us the opportunity to find our audience. Before, I only told jokes in the boys' locker room. I figure I never would have gotten up the courage if you hadn't given me a platform I was already comfortable with, right here with the animals. Now I wonder what else I might rise to, given the encouragement and the chance. Cerise, that offer for dinner still goes, and I promise to tell jokes only if you want me to."

"I accept, Edgar," Cerise replied, her hands pressed together.

The camel driver kicked his heels up and clicked them together, finishing his funny man act with cheers of approval.

The evening started to have a genuine feel-good to it, but Brace's heart literally skipped a beat when Paisley slipped under the "Tunnel of Truth." Ready or not, there she was.

"At what cost is friendship? If we're really going to speak the truth, does it weigh in at a thousand pounds of rhino? Or five ounces of lorikeet?" She took a breath as if to redirect her line of reasoning, sparing him from a record-setting pace for having his heart shredded.

Easing into a seat at the front table to quell his trembling knees, Brace tried to prepare for whatever admission came next.

"What if your new friends cost you an old one? Or took your apartment? What if they made your job next to impossible—and then made it better than ever? Would you look at yourself in the mirror and feel like you've turned a corner? Would you take in a group of gypsies and watch them become your best friends? Could you share what's great about your small town without envying their world experience and wanting it for yourself? One might say we've had a busy summer, letting go of a lot and gaining more than we've given up. Hmmm, that sounds like something supernatural— like God at work in little Pawnee Rock."

With her voice so airy, the hometown name came spoken like something sacred. Brace couldn't argue the fact. He'd gained so much more than he'd given up. Respectability sat chief among them, plus matters of the heart that were whispered in the night. He'd have to give them a voice, if he only could.

"I'm rich for what you've brought into my life," Paisley confessed, knitting her knuckles together. "One of the hometown hosts needs to say this, so let it be me—our home is your home. Don't ever leave, or come back when you can, for all you college students. Like I told Brace that first day—we're your new people. We're nice people, folks who'll take care of you. And lo and behold, in the refraction of God's love, we've received the blessing we first meant for you."

His eyes misted. What more could be said? Christian love ran full circle, and he fell a willing prisoner into the middle of it.

Chapter 22

Head in hands, Brace's tears began to fall. He'd never had a home away from his parents' house. Had never been welcomed outside the parking lot where Re-Occupy was allowed to camp. He'd never been given a chance to make a difference, never been given a job before, never been received by a community with open arms. How completely this felt like God sifting his motives and reasons for staying.

Something soft brushed up against him and there knelt Paisley, enticing him to respond to her with unspoken inquisitions like musical notes in her throat. He took a handful of wispy fabric from her skirt and wiped his eyes. She folded her arms around him and sat next to him. Strength came to him—her strength—and he held her close, quaking.

"I've never felt so loved in my life," a meek female voice claimed. Chloe now stood under the arch, her countenance wholesome and healthy.

No one had come as far as this broken individual, yet she'd been among the first to want to come back that night in the hospital. Paisley's hands slid into his and found a place to nestle it in her lap. Someone sniffed from the far table. The mood had certainly taken a turn for the more serious.

"Don't think it's so easy when you're down and out, because it's harder than you can imagine. It's harder to trust, to allow someone to help or to take shelter from strangers—even if they're well-meaning." Chloe gestured toward Paisley, and she lifted one hand back to connect sister-to-sister over the distance.

Brace thought about how beautiful this truth thing has turned out, giving them an excuse to reach deep inside their hearts to be real instead of living from the shallows. He traced the arch with his gaze and had to stifle a laugh, it stood so rudimentary in its construction. Squinting, the tiny lights danced in celebration as Chloe fought back tears.

"Who'd ever think it could be the Summer of Love for the likes of me?" Chloe seemed to falter and looked away.

"Stay right up there, duet partner," Travis insisted.

Joy-filled with an inkling of what might be coming next, Brace took Paisley's arm and pulled it across his chest for maximum contact.

Travis approached the arch, his western boots clipping the concrete floor with a calypso beat that made his approach more like a dance. "A man can only stay put for so long," he teased, shooting a furtive look at the woman under the arch. Travis offered Chloe his hand and she took it with a delicate touch. "Sweet Chloe Rinehart, secret of my heart's every desire."

The meek woman trembled and placed her other hand over her mouth to keep her astonishment from escaping. Paisley couldn't manage the same and let out a gasp that echoed across the pavilion.

Travis kissed Chloe's forehead and then dropped to one knee, as the tradition so required. Brace felt Paisley sobbing more than heard her and pulled her closer for reinforcement. The world swirled with wonder and they were in it over their heads for the given moment. The harmonica player produced a ring and murmured something personal meant only for his flute player. Face beaming, he focused on her until the positive response came and then slid the ring into place on her slender finger.

Brace turned to give the couple the privacy they deserved for their celebratory embrace, only to find Paisley had done the same. Inches apart, he studied the absolute wonder of the object of his affections as her breath played on his skin. He touched her cheek and the words came to him from above.

"Occupy my heart, Paisley," he whispered, hoping to capture her like a butterfly.

"Already there," she replied with the faintest of candor, right before her lips touched his to prove it. Time stood still behind an arch of twinkling lights.

Truth was love, and Brace had never known it before—but he sure understood it now. Applause trickled up from the back table after a respectable interval of time, and Kurtis crouched to take a picture of the newly engaged couple.

Travis escorted Chloe back to the gang and she showed off the ring with sheer joy.

"Brace wanted to share something with everybody, now that Travis got his twinkling two cents in," Kurtis said, standing under the arch a bit uneasy. Brace tried to mop up his eyes on the back of his hands and stood to join his friend.

"Thanks, Kurtis. I always though going viral meant you were sick, but in our case, it just might make us well. And by us, I mean the wildlife park," Brace clarified. He stole a glance at Paisley and she sat up straighter at the mention of the park. "Chloe, you won't ever know how much change you ushered in the day you shot us out to the electronic world. Even though most of that content ping-pongs around without striking back home, we have some news about what happens when it does.

"As a result of Chloe's YouTube video, we've received an invitation that might bear further consideration. A group called 'Circle Carnival' out of Sarasota, Florida, has invited us to come down and tour through the winter, bringing whatever animals we'd like to include in our performance. There would be a ten-city tour for two weeks a stint. We'd live in RVs, pulling the animal trailers behind us. Let's talk this concept up. How does it strike you? Anybody?"

Paisley was the first to reply. "I think it would help us stay solvent in the winter months when we typically don't have any income at all—only the expense of keeping the animals fed."

"And I could sing year-round," Mimi exclaimed. "That's a dream come true."

"We're slow at the auto shop, so count me in—if Chloe wants to tour Florida, that is," Travis added.

Chloe jumped up and grabbed Mimi, bouncing all around the table like a pair of super balls turned loose.

Lars stood up in the merriment to make his contribution. "We have the longest winter break coming up in school history," he said. "Les and I could ride down and help get the animal cages set up—at least for the first town."

"And maybe come back spring break and help get you moved back up here," Les added.

Edgar rose slowly and seemed a tad less enthusiastic. "Hey guys, I'm not ready to skip town," he admitted. "I've got my second year at the community college and need to stick with it. Maybe I could help with the animals left behind."

"Me, too," Cerise added. "I need to stay closer by my family. I could help Edgar hold down the fort here, if you needed me." She sat back down and Edgar moved toward her, wedging himself beside her at the picnic table.

"How about it, Kurtis?" Brace asked. "How do you see this opportunity?"

"I think it'd be a hoot," he replied, cutting a smile at Mimi. "But something tells me I'd better run this by Steve, being on the ministry team and everything."

Brace saw the wisdom in it. "Fair enough. We'll talk to Steve Wednesday night at supper. We can't let this abandonment by Marty be the end of Tanah Keeta. That much I know. We'll keep searching for ways to pump new life into the park."

"Even if we have to do it from the shade of palm trees," quipped Kurtis. The girl-dance started up beside him again. This time Paisley joined in.

Grateful for the show of support, Brace glanced around the wildlife park committing every detail to memory. This had been the backdrop for the miraculous. He'd never forget it.

~

"No, I can't sanction the Florida proposal and that's

all there is to it," Steve said.

Brace took the blow directly on the sternum as the preacher turned to shake hands with a frail elderly man.

"I'm the shepherd here, and I'm struggling to keep accountability what it should be with you young bucks right here under my nose. But I certainly cannot allow the wildlife park staff to go traipsing all over Florida, with goodness knows what for living arrangements. Now—if the men just want to go, I'm listening."

Kurtis bowed his head, eyeing his guitar case sitting open on the stage. "Travis proposed to Chloe. Guess they'll be getting married before the Florida thing, so he wouldn't leave her for the likes of us."

Brace gritted his teeth at the complication. He understood the moral issues, but wanted to give the new opportunity a fair shake.

"Well, then he's taken the higher road," Steve replied. "Brace, your anointing comes with the admonition to live above reproach as a leader for all things God-centered. Had you given any thought to how it might look for a trio of couples to strike out like that?"

"A man can really only know his own heart, pastor," he replied. "Our intentions were honorable—even if we didn't think the whole thing through."

Steve placed a sympathetic hand on his shoulder, but his expression didn't yield. "No mixed singles are heading to Florida, so Paisley and Mimi are out, understood?"

Brace nodded. Although Mimi might explode in a tantrum of reaction, he truly hated to break the news to Paisley even worse. She would only receive it as getting left behind again. He wasn't sure he could inflict that level of mental agony on someone he loved so much.

When Steve wandered up to the platform, Kurtis shot him a frozen stare that held defiance. "I might just have to see about that higher road," the musician muttered under his breath. He followed Steve and rescued his guitar for opening worship.

In the moment, Brace doubted he could sing with such a heavy heart, but praise came down to a choice. And a broken man could still praise God, even one who'd been denied Florida in the wintertime.

~

"Somebody's being extra quiet tonight," Paisley said, knocking her elbow against Brace's side. The new moon in its no-show yielded stars galore against the sky's black velvet curtain. She could scarcely take it all in.

"Crazy week, I guess," he replied without elaborating.

She felt the brush of his wavy hair against her cheek as he laid his head back on her shoulder. If they hadn't been sitting back-to-back, she'd be giving him a kiss right now. Maybe that would help draw him out. "Yeah, first Travis and Chloe get engaged, and then Kurtis announces his honorable intention to court Mimi. It sure looks like love is on a rampage through the wildlife park. Shoot, they'll all be honeymooning through the Florida circuit if we don't watch out."

"Paisley, we've snagged a glitch with the Florida deal," he replied with flat candor, moving away from her.

A dull ache pulsed from her chest as though her heart had lost its rhythm. "What? Now they don't want us?" Something eerie chaffed the skin on her arms and she passed her hands over them to ward off the evil.

He sat back down across from her and took her hands in his.

Though they were touching, her unease grew and she had a sensation that she was being torn away from Brace. Her stomach churned. She couldn't trust herself to speak. A thousand questions fired off in her head, making the stars disappear in her confusion.

"Out of his protective heart as our shepherd, Steve won't sanction mixed gender single adults going to Florida together." His admission fell flat against the night.

She gasped and looked away sharply, trying to take her hands from him, but he held tight.

"He wants the men to go down, but he forbade us to take Mimi and you."

Her vision soon blurred and the lights from the cars on the Santa Fe Trail below Pawnee Rock became a solid restraining bar of light—a laser prison.

"So Kurtis and Mimi?" she asked, wiping her nose on her sleeve. Maybe focusing on others would eventually bring them to the matter at hand.

"He's not willing to split up his duet, for more reasons than one," Brace replied.

She tried not to read anything into the pause that followed, but it became obvious what he wasn't saying about their teamed performance—and their relationship.

"He's hopeful that, by the end of the year, they might be ready to tie the knot like Travis and Chloe."

The knife stabbing her side couldn't let her think clearly, as two of the three couples spawned by Re-Occupy seemed to be having a lasting effect. Naturally, hers would be the one that faltered. The knife blade twisted at that recognition, like something needed to be scraped off her heart. Perhaps it was her self-sufficiency.

"We're different, I know," she said weakly, trying not to sound like a defeated sop. "We have more responsibility for the wildlife park, so I should stay, really. With no director right now, we don't know how this public ownership thing will work out."

He pulled away and ran his hands through his hair before tumbling forward into a somersault. That led to a maddening fit of round-offs across the pavilion's roof in the plain sight of God and a hundred thousand celestial beings. He came back walking on his hands as though the upside-down position best fit the mood of their conversation. "Paisley, what Steve calls 'the higher road' won't work for us," he finally admitted out of breath.

She had never heard break-up words expressed more effectively. She tried not to be shocked, but it took every ounce of restraint she possessed. Though blindsided by the emotional trauma, the Spirit within her cried out to God. He who pledged to never leave or forsake her would have to come to her rescue yet again. When the dull ache of failure split her brow, thinking through the situation became out of the question.

Brace squatted but refused to connect by withholding his touch. Now even that had been taken away.

The knife stuck in to the hilt, leaving her half-alive. "It's okay, Brace. No pressure. Better to honor God in the long run than be irresponsible with a short-term fling." That hurt to admit, but she had to let him off the hook.

He laughed and slung something off the rooftop. It

may as well have been her heart. "Paisley St. James," he said, reproof tingeing his voice. When she could finally bear to look at him, he was kneeling in front of her on both knees, folding his hands prayerfully. He tilted his head enough for the security light to flood his face and his eyes pooled with emotion. "I love you with every inch of my heart. I thank God for that every morning, noon, and night because I wasn't looking for it, but love found me right here at Pawnee Rock. I look at you and I want to soar out above the treetops like a lorikeet." A single tear leaked onto his cheek.

Though his words spoke of love, there didn't seem to be any available for her. "But there's no higher road for us?" she questioned, needing an explanation to appease her sanity. If he truly loved her, why couldn't it take them to the higher road unless, of course, he didn't find her proper marriage material? She wasn't dainty like Chloe or petite like Mimi. That perspective pierced deeper than the knife. Death by body type—not even Shakespeare could have come up with that tragedy.

"I can't...take you into my debt, Paisley. It's my burden to bear and I need...more time to pay it down," he confessed, looking into her eyes.

The need to move hit her like a violent wind, unrelenting with its insistence. She lunged off the bench, twirled into a dance move and set her hair free in the wind. Full of passion, she thrashed against the circumstance and shattered all the sedentary forces holding her back. Circling the overlook, she threw off any sense of pride or selfish concern.

Halting at the top of the spiral staircase, she froze when a possible solution came to her. So full of light, she knew it must be from God.

The gymnast stepped to her, his chest heaving against hers in expectation. He lifted a hand and stroked her hair like a phantom admirer, unable to stake his claim for the future.

She'd be bold enough to stake it for him—if God would only allow her the very words a proper woman must never speak. "Brace Cordan, would you—with infinite love over the treetops—marry me at my heart's earnest begging?"

His hands found her shoulders with a tremble, so close she could hear his labored breath.

"Would you allow me the honor of sharing your load of debt, so we could make it disappear in half the time? And would you allow me the joy of sharing each day with you, no matter where we go? Marry me, Ace, and make me the happiest woman in the world." As far out on the limb as she could get, she'd have to give him a few seconds to mull over her offer, hard though it would be.

He sobbed and tried to swallow it down, clearing his throat to regain control. "Paisley," he responded, his voice full of longing. "What is it about you that makes the whole world so… loveable?" His fingertips found her jaw and traced a line to her cheekbone as though to prove she really existed.

To lure him in with a kiss seemed so…underhanded. Taking a deep breath, the stars came back into the sky behind them like the aura of the Almighty. Everything held its focus and her heart waited to be claimed in the night breeze. "One shouldn't answer a question with another question." Growing anxious for an answer, her knees started to tremble.

A sturdy arm slipped around her back. "I want to

court you like a madman," he replied, his voice level and sure. "Then I want to marry you by the holidays. Say you will, and be my swirly-girl for all time."

Before she could answer, he kissed her to sweeten the offer. She let the seal of his intentions set like wax drying on fine parchment. Once the opportunity presented itself, she settled the issue. "Yes, I will, because love *is* the higher road."

"Pastor Steve will be so happy to find you in agreement," he replied. Then he hoisted her toward the night sky and they began to spin together under the stars, part gymnastics act and part freeform dance, a truly selfless blend of forward movement.

Epilogue

The crisp autumn day smelled of persimmons and pumpkins as the church door flew open to release the newlyweds. Corn husk and paper-twist ribbons held sprigs of bittersweet along the railings as Paisley drank in the light of day as an emerging bride. Brace stepped beside her and offered his arm as they fought the well-intentioned spray of birdseed all the way to their carriage. A peek over her shoulder revealed Kurtis taking Mimi up in his arms to shoulder through the assault amid her lighthearted giggles.

Turning for the last carriage, she watched Travis bring Chloe down the steps, supporting her like a fragile bride-doll. With so much joy wrapped around so many fulfillments, Paisley thought her heart would melt. Brace gestured toward the steed and she spotted the camel from the wildlife park. Laughing, she pulled at his tux collar and inhaled, the sparkling blue eyes of her groom speaking an invitation only for her.

"Let's take it slow over to the pavilion," she said as his hands found her waist. Up into the carriage she went, launched by the muscular arms of an aerialist.

"I don't think we have any choice," he replied, saluting to Edgar and climbing inside. The animal trainer tipped his top hat and slapped the reins from the driver's seat, starting them off on the first leg of their life adventure together. In seconds, Steve appeared at the end of the churchyard, tossing a final handful of seed as they huddled together laughing. Children clapped as Steve gestured skyward and Paisley realized she only had one direction left to go—and that was up to the unwavering Pawnee Rock.

The End

ABOUT THE AUTHOR

Nature writer Cindy M. Amos incorporates familiar landscapes into her plot-driven romance stories. Having moved inland from the Atlantic coast, she walks the meadows of the tallgrass prairie on the Amos family ranch in the incomparable Flint Hills of Kansas, studying nature and searching for her next inspiration. Intrigued by the notch of Dakota sandstone poking the horizon along the Santa Fe Trail, she chose Pawnee Rock as the immovable setting for *Sanctifying Ace Aerialist*. With Landscapes of Mercy as her debut series, Ms. Amos writes from Wichita, Kansas where she shares a home with her aviation industry husband and two come-and-go college-aged sons. The wildlife park theme was borrowed from her celebration of "the last golden day of summer" with her youngest son, a suggestion from Winnie the Pooh taken fondly to heart.

Read more about the author on her website at http://cindymamos.wixsite.com/natureink.

<u>OTHER BOOKS BY CINDY M. AMOS</u>

LANDSCAPES OF MERCY SERIES

Book One   *Redeeming River Rancher*

Book Two   *Saving Bicycle Man*

Book Three   *Justifying Sound Strider*

NATIONAL PARK ROMANCE SERIES

Everglades Entanglement